STYLES P

INVINCIBLE

A NOVEL

ONE WORLD TRADE PAPERBACKS

BALLANTINE BOOKS | NEW YORK

One World Books Trade Paperback Original

Copyright © 2010 by The Phantom Entertainment, Inc.

Published in the United States by One World Books,
an imprint of The Random House Publishing Group,
a division of Random House, Inc., New York.

ONE WORLD is a registered trademark and the One World colophon is a
trademark of Random House, Inc.

ISBN 978-0-345-50752-5

Printed in the United States of America

www.oneworldbooks.net

4 6 8 9 7 5

Book design by Laurie Jewell

This book is dedicated to my father
and my brother. Rest in peace.

To my mother, for instilling the love
of books in me.

To my wife, for pushing me forward,
and for the energy and inspiration
to knock it out.

Love all of y'all.

A NOTE FROM NIKKI TURNER

My Dearest Readers,

Thanks once again for all your undying support over so many years. Without you none of this would be possible. So, to give back, I feel it's only right to continue introducing you to great new books, and let me be the first to say: This book you are holding in your hand is going to far exceed all expectations you may have.

Styles P had already mastered the music game, so I knew his book would be a treat. I had been a fan of Styles and the Lox long before I was approached to publish his book under the Nikki Turner Presents umbrella. I knew he was a wonderful lyrical talent, but I honestly had no idea that the international rapper, artist, actor, dad, and dog breeder would put the same passion into this book that he regularly puts into his music.

In the very early stages of work on *Invincible*, Styles mentioned to me that he breeds dogs, and I shared with him the tragic story of my Yorkie, Mr. Biggs, whom I'd just lost. He told me that I needed a pit bull in my life and once he found one with the right temperament, he was going to give me a puppy. I didn't think much more about it until months later, when he called to tell me he had the perfect dog for me. I was shocked. I didn't take him seriously at the time, nor was I really the pit bull type of girl, either. I accepted the dog, and Glitz has totally won my heart over. So, I have to thank Styles for adding such a great addition to my family.

Now, as the process continued, I would ask Styles how the writing was coming, and he'd respond to me that he was writing—ON HIS SIDEKICK! In all my days in the writing game I'd never encountered anyone who had written a *chapter* on a Sidekick, let alone an entire *book*. I thought it was the craziest thing ever, but when he sent me the first few chapters, not only was I sucked in, but I found an entirely new level of respect for him. His story was such an amazing read, and after finishing it, I felt that *Invincible* is what urban fiction is really about—an action packed gangsta film with characters who stay with you long after you turn the last page.

After you put down this book, I know you'll agree that Styles P is an amazing talent, and you will be sitting on the edge of your seat waiting for part two.

So, without further ado, I present to you . . . *Invincible*.

Enjoy!

Much Love,
Nikki Turner

PROLOGUE

Jake couldn't help but feel like he was carrying the weight of the world on his shoulders. His legs had given out, and he felt like an animal being led to slaughter. The stench from the back of the cop car and the pain in his wrists and shoulders from being cuffed so tight was unbearable. What little faith Jake had in mankind had just disappeared.

Two men robbed Kim and his store and took what was his ($$$$$), and yet *he* was the one in the back of the police car. Sure, Jake knew it was foolish to go and shoot the robbers, but deep down he understood that what comes around goes around, and he had done enough dirt to last for two lifetimes. The wiser thing to do would've been to let the robbers bounce without giving chase, but he just couldn't control himself.

Maybe it was his past that drove him to squeeze the trigger, but as he fired his gun and felt it kick and saw the flame from the barrel, he knew exactly where he was headed—p-r-i-s-o-n. In his world, there was no such thing as fair play—not from the thieves, not from the police, not from women, not from family or so-called friends. As far as Jake was concerned, only God could be trusted. Jake learned at an early age not to trust anyone else, a lesson he learned from the so-called closest people in the world to him: his parents. Jake's father was a crackhead and his churchgoing mother never seemed to care what he did or which streets he ran, making Jake question her love. His uncle was cool but had introduced Jake to some shit a child shouldn't be involved with, leading Jake to believe as he grew older that in life you're always gonna need somebody else, but all you really have is yourself.

The back of the cop car made it clear to Jake that he was headed back to hell and his gut feeling told him only God could help him now.

CHAPTER 1

TRUST NO ONE

County jail dorm, January 2008

Except for minimum activity the dorm was mostly quiet at this hour. There was no chatter among the mostly new faces, no questions from cats awaiting sentencing, no more trading war stories or survival tips—the smell was the only thing that was loud. It was a little after three in the morning and the drugs-infested, gang-riddled jail had taken on an almost serene glow when Jake dropped to his knees to pray. At times like this it didn't matter that he felt his prayers were never answered in the past; old routines were hard to break. Jake slowly rose from his praying position, allowing his eyes to scan the dorm; most everyone appeared to be asleep. The tier gave off its usual cacophony of noises for this time of the night: loud snoring, fart trumpets, and sounds of nightmares of terror coming from some of the guys who were probably locked up for the first time and scared shitless. *How the fuck did I get myself back in this position again,* Jake thought. Then the realism of the situation punched him slam in the face: His lifestyle put him here. In order to make himself feel a fraction better he rationalized that everything happened for a reason and God knew better than he what those reasons were. But he still asked God the same thing he always asked when he was in a fix: "Please get me out of here," followed by the other shit he always said: "I swear I'll chill this time!"

After waiting patiently for the CO to make his ring, Jake shoved his index finger into the hole he had made inside of the waistband of his boxers and fished out a neatly rolled stick of kush. He licked it, lit it, took a few quick pulls and held the smoke in his lungs as long as he could. When he finally exhaled, he got a bottle of baby powder and blew three handfuls of it into the air to cover the smell before concealing the remainder of the spliff back in its hiding place.

Jake looked around one last time and was cool about his surroundings. He lay down in his bunk and went to sleep with one eye open!

CHAPTER 2

BAD NEWS

"Jake Billings!" It was CO Frazier yelling from the front of the dorm. "Jake Billings," he repeated. "Come get your mail before the garbage gets it."

Jake walked to the CO desk with a little pep in his step because he knew CO Frazier would do exactly what he said he would do. When he got to the desk, Frazier tossed the mail at him along with a do-you-want-a-problem-motherfucker look. Jake picked his mail up off the floor and kept moving; he knew better than to feed into the corrections officer's bullshit. He didn't need any extra problems right now. He'd been in jail for five days and hadn't gotten in contact with anyone yet. To keep it one hundred he wasn't expecting any mail in the first place; he was waiting on a visit from his girl so he could put her up on what he needed to get out of there.

Sitting back on his bunk, Jake looked over the envelope he'd just gotten: no return address or name. Not really in the mood for surprises, he ripped the envelope open and read:

Dear J.B. you don't know me, but I know you or rather I know of you, and you can't believe how happy I am to see you in this jail. I'm sending you this kite to let you know I am going to fucking kill you. Your best bet is to check into PC you bitch-ass nigga. You violated the wrong nigga many moons ago and what comes around goes around motherfucka. I hope you're built for war.

Oh and p.s.
Praying in the middle of the night ain't gonna help a fucking thing.

> *Sincerely yours,*
> *Real Nigga, Same Dorm*

Internally, Jake was fucked up knowing that a nigga was not only watching him but wanted him dead, and he had no idea who that nigga was, but he wouldn't give anything away to his stalker. Jake had mastered the art of being emotionally cold many years ago; therefore, he hadn't a worry in the world of his expression or body language giving him away.

The fact that an anonymous person had sent him a heads-up that they wanted him dead meant one of two things to Jake: He was stupid for tipping his hand and had no idea how dangerous Jake was, or he was the real deal and wanted to play mind games before murder games. Either way, Jake appreciated the letter for putting him on point. But he didn't appreciate his life being threatened, or being called a bitch-ass nigga.

Who would want to see him dead? He thought for a second, but who was he kidding—his list of enemies was as long as Broadway. He needed to concentrate on what he did know, and that was that whoever wrote the letter was more than likely watching. Jake decided to put on a show for his anonymous audience. He strolled over to the trash, crumbled the letter with a smile on his face, and threw it in the can. Satisfied with the production, he went to his bin and got out a towel, toothbrush, soap, and boxers. Then he came out of his county oranges and walked to the shower whistling, as if he didn't have a care in the world. *I can play mind games, too,* he thought, as he walked toward the shower with his head up, chest out, and sneakers on.

"Billings," the CO yelled out. "You got a V.I. I see you about to hop in the shower so I'm going to give you five minutes to do what you gotta do before you come get this pass. Washing your ass is the smartest thing you done since you been here," he joked. "Now hurry the fuck up."

Ignoring the CO, Jake stepped into the shower wondering if his bold act at the trash can was a wise one or if his pride would lead to his demise—only time would tell.

He quickly began soaping up his 6'1", 240-pound body. Once he felt like his body was good and clean, he soaped up his mid-brown bald head. Beads of hot water bounced off the tense muscles that made up his broad back, which was cut up from previous bids and frequent visits to the pull-up bar in the park by his crib. Jake felt he could handle himself with just about anyone, but who said it was going to be only one person when the attack came. However, the attack hadn't come yet; no one followed him or came in during his shower so he hurried to catch his V.I.

Jake got dressed and went and got the pass from the CO, then headed toward the electric door—waiting for the CO in the bubble to open it. While he waited, Jake took a good look around for any faces he might recognize, but the problem was that there were too many faces he'd seen before. The doors in jail revolve like a carousel from hell . . . same niggaz in and out with new ones always joining the ride. He would have to deal with this shit after his visit. The CO in the bubble popped the gate and Jake stepped out into the hallway.

"Let me see your pass," the CO working the hall asked. Everywhere an inmate went in the jail there was a CO. This was what they called controlled movement. Jake showed his pass to the CO and waited for the elevator. Right now the only thing on his mind was how come it took his girl five days to come visit him. *Something ain't right*, he thought.

Kim was running out of patience as she sat waiting in the visiting room for Jake. She knew he wasn't in control of the time or movement in the jail, but she was still pissed off at him like it was his fault. Kim chuckled to herself. She noticed she stood out like a black sheep among a herd of white ones in the visiting room: Most of the women visiting their men had a look of stress or concern on their faces and looked tired and de-pressed. Kim had none of those problems. *I ain't stressed or the least bit concerned with Jake's future at the moment, and definitely don't look tired and depressed like these bitches.* Kim felt and looked like a million bucks. Every man who walked into the visiting room couldn't help but notice her, and every one of their girls couldn't help but roll her eyes at her.

Kim was 5'10" with a mocha complexion and the body of a runner, the face of a goddess, and the mind and heart of a cold, calculated criminal. Kim had purposely waited a week before she came to see Jake. She wanted him to be uncomfortable and riled up. She wanted to ruffle his feathers for once. He always acted so cool, and she hated that about him. Kim was glad he was in jail, honestly. Now she could do all she wanted without consequence.

Kim told herself she really did love Jake; after all, he was one of the realest men she'd ever met. But it was over between them—finally. They had gotten as far as they could as a couple and had made decent money, but the past couple of years their relationship had gotten kind of rocky and Jake was no longer fitting in Kim's plans. So him shooting those dudes in the store was right up her alley. *This is my way out. I got too much shit to do. I rode out with this nigga every other time he was locked up, but not this time. Now I'm gonna do me.*

Kim was psyching herself up to handle her business. *Fuck this nigga he don't fit in with my plans. We have different agendas, and it is time for me to move on.*

Kim once again had to chuckle to herself. It was really funny how she was planning to get away from Jake. And he only had himself to blame. *He is the one who made me into the monster I am today.*

———

Kim and Jake had known each other practically their whole lives. They were both raised by churchgoing mothers and went to the same schools throughout elementary, junior high, and high school, but they never went out with each other until they were nineteen. It started one day when Kim was going to community college and J.B. was going to his spot to knock off his work for the day. J.B. kept a spot by the school for several reasons. One was that he didn't like hustling crack on the same block where he laid his head, and another was that it was easy to knock off a pound of weed in about a week around there. College kids love to get high.

Kim was about to walk by when Jake got the idea to stop her. He had been thinking about making her a proposition for a while now and today was as good as any.

"Hey, Kim, what's up?" he called to her. "Can I talk to you for a sec?"

"Sure, what up, Jay?"

"I've been meaning to run a few things by you."

"Okay, shoot."

"Do you go to work somewhere after school?" he asked, already knowing the answer to his question because he had been keeping an eye on Kim for a while.

"I wish I did."

"Then your wish just came true. I got some work for you."

Kim knew that Jake dabbled in a lot of different illegal things so when she asked what, and he told her, she responded, "I can't sell weed, J.B.," almost too loudly. "I wouldn't even know what to do or say. Plus, I can't afford to get kicked out of school."

Jake laughed. "You don't have to do it in school and you don't have to say much. The customer will do most of the talking." After getting her attention with that, he gave her the run-down. "See, I have this apartment around the corner where the students come to cop from. The problem is I don't have the time to be in there from four to ten because I have a lot of running around to do—I need some help. All you got to do is sit in the apartment and when they knock, tell them to slide the money under the door. We only sell dimes so you can figure out what to give them. I will return every day around ten P.M. to relieve you."

Kim stood there seriously considering Jake's offer. God knows she could use the extra money. Her school books alone were costing her a fortune, and that was for the used ones, but she still had a few other concerns. "What if somebody tries to rob me?"

Jake gave her a smile that said he had it all under control. "The whole transaction is made under the door," he said. "It's more than enough space; I had the bottom of the door shaved so that there's no reason to ever open it up. Trust me."

"What about police?" she asked, covering all bases.

Jake put his cards on the table and spoke to her earnestly. "Well that's another story. If the police kick this shit in you're going to jail, but you will only be in there a couple of hours. Weed ain't no felony and being that you're a girl the most they'll hit you with is a fine and a warning to stay out of trouble for a year."

When she asked how much money she'd make, Jake knew that she was down. He told her she would make three dollars off of every ten-dollar bag that she sold.

"How about four?" she cracked.

Jake laughed. "The job is only worth two dollars a bag," he said. "I'm being generous with three."

"Why don't you find someone else?" she asked honestly.

" 'Cause I've known you for a long time and I don't have to worry about you doing any grimy shit. And besides, our moms are friends and I know y'all going through hard times right now so I figured this could help both of us!"

She told him to let her sleep on it and she would let him know tomorrow, although she already knew the answer was yes. There were just too many bills in her household and she needed some kind of income.

Tomorrow came around and she told him it was cool with her. He chilled with her for the first few hours so he could walk her through the process. "It's simple," he explained. "You hear the knock . . . tell them to slide the dough . . . you slide the smoke—everything is done. The door is double bolted so you're safe, and if something goes wrong I'll be right down the block. Plus, I got somebody keeping their eye on the spot."

"Do you mind if I ask what you're doing down the block that's so important that you're not here collecting your own money?" she asked.

"I'm down there knocking off base; that's where the real money is."

"Don't you feel funny selling that stuff knowing what it does?"

Jake knew that she was referring to the fact that his father was a crackhead. "Yeah, I feel a certain kind of way being that my pops is a basehead, but I'll feel even funnier being broke with a basehead pops. Plus I'm only gonna do this hustling shit until I can save enough to buy a clothing store and a laundromat. After that I'm going to find the flyest chick in the city and have kids and move out of this shit. That's my plan, what's yours?"

"I'm going to graduate and move my moms outta here," Kim said. "I have a boyfriend who goes to school in Cali. Maybe I will go there, I don't know yet."

"You got a man in Cali?" J.B. asked kinda shocked. "Ain't that kinda far? Why don't you get yourself a nice New York college boy?"

"I haven't met one yet."

"I got a homie." J.B. sort of smiled. "He's in college and he's cool. I think you might like him."

"No thanks, J.B." she said returning his smile. "I always knew there was something crazy about you ever since we were young. You never paid attention to anyone. You were always in your own world—very rebellious but still very kind. Now here you are offering me a job and a nice college friend. I hope I don't look like I need handouts. What is my moms telling your moms anyway?"

"Damn girl, chill out! I told you you were cool so I felt a'ight telling you about this shit. All my closest friends are way outta town or not around, plus I know you kinda stay to yourself so that works for me. If you were a bird I wouldn't have asked you to join my empire." J.B. laughed, and so did Kim.

———

The elevator opened.

"Ooohhhhh shit, J.B., nah nigga—not you!" It was his homie Reggie from high school. "Damn, nigga, I ain't seen you since Lord knows. I heard you owned a clothing store with mix tapes and the whole shit . . . fly mommies helping niggaz and all that. What brings you to hell this time, my nigga?"

"Attempted murder," Jake told his friend. Seeing the look on his old friend's face, he explained, "Two niggaz in the store start beefing with each other over Lord knows what, next thing I know guns come out. Nobody was shooting, just yelling and aiming at each other. I was trying to tell them chill out but they just kept yelling. Next thing I know one of 'em turned around and told me to get on the floor. His partner told the girls to do the same and then walked to the front door and locked it. Niggaz was on some real-life movie shit, son. When they told me to open the safe I popped that shit open for 'em with no hesitation. After I handed the dude all the money, they took off for the door. Where the smart mu'fuckaz fucked up at is they never bothered to search the girls for a burner . . . they only searched me. My girls are required to tote at all times, so I grabbed one of their tools, ran out behind the cowards sparking off. Hit 'em both: one in the leg and the other in the shoulder. Next thing I heard was 'get on the floor,' which brings me here."

"Damn, J.B., how much cash you kept in the safe?" Reggie asked, genuinely sorry about the bad one his old friend took.

"Two hundred thou," Jake said, "which the police stole from them. So now I'm beat for the paper and I got a case."

"I thought you could pop a nigga for trying to rob your property, ain't that a law or some shit?"

"It probably is, Regg, but on paper I don't own the store— I'm just an employee. If I was down as the owner the feds would've been on my ass about where I got the loot to buy a store."

The bell in the elevator went off. "Okay," the CO said. "The ride's over."

They all got off. "Where they got you housed at, my nigga?" Reggie asked.

"Third floor—northwest side . . . How about you, Regg?"

"Second floor—southeast side. I got the shit on smash, too! I got pull in this bitch. Ain't shit changed from the streets. You know me. I'm all about that paper. You wanna get moved to my block I can make it happen."

"Nah, Regg, I got some shit to handle. If I don't see you coming off the V.I., I'll kite you in a few."

"No doubt, J.B. Hate to see you in here but it is good to see you. Holla if you need something. One!"

Jake still had to go through the rest of the usual routine that the jail made all inmates go through before their visits: drop your drawers, lift your nuts, turn around and split your ass cheeks, show the bottoms of your feet, open your mouth—and after all that they still gave him a small-ass jumpsuit.

When Jake stepped into the visiting room, despite how overcrowded it was, he spotted his girl right away and walked to her table. She stood up to greet him with a cold hug and short kiss, then they both sat down.

"I'm pretty sure you knew I was locked up like five days ago. What took you so long to get here, Kim?" Jake cracked right off the bat. "I know we ain't been on the best of terms but if it's going to be like this maybe it's best that we come to some sort of agreement right now!"

"Nigga please, you should be lucky that I'm here at all with yo grimy ass," Kim shot right back. "The store—*my* store, since it's in my name—is fine, like all the rest of my properties."

That's why I've been doing all my shit on the side anyway. I knew you weren't reliable for shit in the long run, she thought. "What I came to do is be a courteous bitch and have the decency to let you know you're on your own on this trip. Don't expect a visit, a letter, or anything from me. I'm through with you and I don't want you thinking I'm going to be here for you when I'm not. Don't get me wrong, I love you, but I'm not in love anymore. I've dealt with seven years of your bullshit and now I'm through. I came to relay any messages you have for your lawyers or workers."

Jake wanted to reach across the table and choke the bitch for coming off at him the way she did but that would get him nowhere. "Thanks for letting me know what was up," he said instead. "I'm sorry things got so bitter between us in the past two years, but I didn't know you felt this way. If I did I would've let you out of your misery a long time ago, baby." Jake kept his eyes locked with hers. "And as far as needing your help for anything, I'm all right. I can help myself out." He told her "Good luck" before getting up and walking toward the CO, leaving her sitting at the table with a face that looked mad, sad, and confused all at once.

The nerve of this nigga, she thought. Her plans were to leave him upset and somehow he managed to flip it on her. She wound up being the upset one. "He really doesn't give a fuck," was all she kept saying to herself. A single tear escaped her eye and ran down her cheek as she left the visiting room thinking: *He's really crazy . . . all of these years for nothing.*

J.B. felt like this had to be the worst day of his life. He hated to be so cold to Kim but the fact was he was in a situation and she wasn't riding. Then there was that other business. There was a chance he might not make it out of this one. Something didn't feel right and he wasn't sure if he played his hand right with Regg earlier. Could Reggie be the enemy? Could the police have planted the letter? One thing he did know was that when he got back to that block anybody who got within arm's length of him was going to have a problem. If today was his day, he was going out hard-body style.

CHAPTER 3

STANDING TALL

When Jake was escorted back to his block after leaving the visiting area, he did the same thing he'd been doing since his incarceration five days ago. He sat on the edge of his bunk and read anything and everything he could get his hands on. Reading usually helped to clear his head, but for some reason it wasn't working for him today. Having read the same newspaper three times probably had something to do with it. Besides, who was he fooling; his mind was still on that crazy letter he got earlier. Peeking over the top of the sports section, he scoped the block for anyone who appeared to be watching him, and it seemed like everyone was watching. Fuck this. Tired of sitting around waiting, Jake decided to do some shit that hopefully would throw the mystery letter writer far left. He sprang off the bunk and stepped toward the garbage can that was kept near the back of the block. When he got there he called for the trustee. "Yo, let me get the gloves." The trustee had a puzzled look on his face but knew better than to ask questions. Jail wasn't the place to blatantly mind another man's business. The trustee went to his bunk and came back with what Jake asked for. Jake slid the thick rubber gloves on and began to rummage through the garbage can. It didn't take him long to find what he was looking for. Part one of his plan accomplished, Jake returned the gloves to the trustee and headed back to his sleeping area to pack his stuff.

Everything he owned was stored in a bin and kept under the bunk. In no hurry, he transferred the items from the bin to his laundry bag. Even taking his time it only took a couple of minutes to get his belongings together. Shower shoes, towel, soap, deodorant, writing paper, a pencil, a couple of magazines and newspapers and he was done. They weren't allowed to have much, and he had even less.

He laid his bag on his bunk and walked over to the TV area. Half the dorm was sitting in front of the television watching a college basketball game. If he was going to be getting the business while he was here, he would give a little, too. Jake turned the television off and addressed all who were listening. "Whichever one of you gentlemen want a problem with me"— he looked at each man sitting and standing before him—"when the CO makes his ring . . . play the bathroom. Bring your shank, your homeboy, whatever it is you're into . . . other than that I'm tryin' to chill. But I ain't into no niggaz sending me threatening letters like some sweet nigga. I'm use to bitches doing that shit—not real niggaz! And for a little extra incentive . . . anybody who gives me the info on which faggot wrote this letter there's a five-hundred-dollar commissary award. Sorry to interrupt y'all niggaz show!" Then he put the TV back on and started to walk to his bunk, but before he got there Jake got a couple of buyers on the tickets he'd just sold.

They were two of the biggest dudes in the dorm, and they weren't feeling Jake pushing that macho shit in their block. "Fuck you put your hands on my TV for?" one of them asked, followed by a looping right hand.

Jake bobbed the punch but got caught with a short jab from the first guy's partner. *Maybe that move was a wrong one,* Jake thought. This wasn't the beef he was looking for. Neither one of these guys was likely to be the mystery letter writer, but he had no choice but to use the situation to his advantage. Without much more thought about it, Jake started to do one of the things he did best . . . cause pain.

The two brawlers were getting the best of Jake, but that would soon change. He started timing the one on his right who was laying stomps. He was slow, but if one of them size four-teens caught him right, Jake figured it would be lights out for him. The guy on the left was trying to punch him in the head. *What an idiot,* Jake thought. *He could've broken my ribs already.* When the internal counter in his head said "now," Jake grabbed the leg of the dude who was trying to stomp him out. Before the dude ever knew what had happened, Jake had taken a bite out of his Achilles tendon like it was a piece of chicken. Bingo!

Big man dropped to the floor. One down and one to go. All the squats and crunches Jake did helped him to spring off the floor back onto his feet, quickly leaving him squared up with the big headhunter. Jake shot two quick left jabs at him that not only connected, but left the big man stunned, though only for a second. He snapped out of it and rushed Jake with a wide, right-handed head shot. Jake sidestepped the wild punch and let loose his own right-left combo to the body. The gut-wrenching blows would have dropped a normal human being, but big man ate the blows then resorted to the wrestling thing. Grabbing Jake wasn't the smartest move to make. By now, big man was banged up and too tired to slam Jake. Jake delivered a vicious head butt and gave big man a floor spot next to his man with the ate-up Achilles.

Jake was breathing hard and trying to catch his breath to prepare for the ass whipping he was about to receive. The CO in the booth had probably pulled his pin alerting the turtles—the Fuck You Up Squad, as the inmates liked to call those cops in their riot gear—to come shut down whatever and whoever the problem was. No turtles showed though, just CO Frazier. He was walking toward the three men laughing as if he just heard the funniest joke in the world. "You fucking punks got some nerve lying on the floor like two bitches in a doghouse," CO Frazier admonished. "All that extorting and tough-guy shit y'all been pulling on everybody. Today wasn't y'all day, huh? I tell you what—I got two passes on the desk for you assholes to go to the nurse and get your shit fixed up. Tell her some bullshit story you would have told police or the DA, but I ain't see shit and I'm pretty sure you two tough guys ain't rats, right?" Not waiting for or expecting an answer, CO Frazier turned his attention to Jake. "Billings," he said in a stern voice, "at my desk . . . Now!"

Jake followed Frazier to his desk thinking: *This guy sho is different from the usual CO.*

Once they were at the desk, CO Frazier got straight to the point. "Billings, I don't know if you noticed but this is my house and I ain't gonna stand for your cowboy shit. The two assholes you just beat up were scumbags for sure, but they didn't bring attention to my house. They did all the shit on the low: extortion, rape, drugs, whatever it is they do, but they were quiet about it. The usual CO works their dorm for eight hours of the day. Not me, Billings, I'm in here for two shifts. That means when you lock down for the count or, in this case, stay on your bunk for the count, and when you wake back up, I'm still here. And I don't want no fucking captain coming in here telling me shit, or asking me shit about my house. Now Ike and Cory ain't gonna take that ass whipping like men even though they tried to jump you. Next time they come at you it's going to be with weapons or with more flunkies. In case you didn't know, this is a gang-infested jail . . . the Money Boys, the Northside Boys, the Spanish Crowns, and the 300 Crew . . . and you just fucked up two Northside soldiers. Which means you're fucked. So I'm going to tell the captain to send you to PC when he comes around."

"Whoa, Whoa, Whoa," Jake spoke up. "With all due respect I would prefer to stay right here. I'm a man and it is too many fags and funny shit going on in protective custody. Leave me here and I will deal with whatever I have to deal with. I don't give a fuck about no gangs, and besides, I won't be here too much longer anyway. I got court in a few days and then I'm bailing outta this joint."

Jake attempted to go back to the dorm but CO Frazier put up his hand like a flagger, stopping him from getting by. "Listen young-blood." The CO got Jake's attention. "You ain't gonna make it in this house, them motherfuckas will kill you! Yeah, I see you can fight, but you don't want the kinda problems you're about to have."

"Just let me handle me, please. I'll be a'ight," Jake said, and just as he did, rec was announced across the PA system.

"Okay, you can go," CO Frazier said against his better judgment. "But I'm going to keep an eye on you."

The whole dorm, minus Ike and Cory, flew out the door. Some to spread the word on what happened in their house, some to buy or sell drugs, and some just to kick it with a homie housed somewhere else. For the five days Jake was in the jail he didn't go out. Today that would change!

The yard and the kitchen were prime spots for drama to go down in jail because those were the places where inmates could link up with their buddies who weren't in the same block as them. After the rumble on the block, Jake was mentally prepared to go all out as he stepped into the yard. His only problem was that he needed a weapon: that's why he was trying to spot Reggie, which didn't take long. Reggie came up to him mad excited. "What up nigga, you a'ight? I heard you was putting it down!"

Jake gave Reggie the whole story, beginning with the letter he got before going on the visit, and ending with the fight and conversation he'd just had with CO Frazier.

"That's why I need the shank," he said. "If I can't get that I'll take some batteries, and if all else fails I'll just have to resort to the old soap-in-the-sock shit."

Reggie told him to slow down, before adding, "Them Northside niggaz is pussy but they deep in numbers." Reggie then let him know that he was one of the founding members of the Money Boys and that he and a few of the Northside leaders was cool . . . so he would squash the beef. "Besides, there a few niggaz in T.M.B. that's housed in the same joint as you. I already gave them the word to hold you down from anything that's unfair. If a nigga wants you he gotta come head up, my nigga."

Jake thanked Reggie for holding him down but politely declined any other help besides the weapon that he asked for.

Reggie wouldn't take no for an answer. "Too late, the word is already in, but I'll still give you the banger if that'll make you feel better. I can get it to you before rec is over, my nigga, but I also got to let you know that your block is gonna get a shake tomorrow night and you don't wanna get knocked with what I'm going to give you. I ain't got no jail bullshit. I got real knives, nigga. I told you I got shit on smash in this spot. If you decide to move to my block then whatever you need we can get . . . cellphones, real food, drugs, a li'l pussy every now and then, the fly kicks before they come out, mix tapes or whatever." Reggie could tell Jake was impressed by the way he was looking at him so he continued to brag. "Yeah nigga, everything in here gets ran by an elite group of men and you're talking to one of those men."

While Reggie was talking Jake noticed there were a lot of people walking toward where he and Jake were standing. Jake clenched both fists—prepared to rock—as the group approached. Reggie peeped the tension in Jake and told him to chill, but Jake wasn't feeling the situation.

It was a group of Northside Boys, wanting to know why the Money Boys was minding their business. They also wanted to meet the nigga who single-handedly broke up two of their top soldiers. Leading the group were two kids who went by the names Lil Red and Dollar Bill, kids who just happened to be blood brothers. Lil Red, the short stocky one, spoke first. "Listen, Regg, we cool but you can't try to hold this one down. That nigga went into a Northside house and caused trouble. We can't afford to tolerate that type of activity. Next thing you know we got all kinds of niggaz trying to pull the same shit because they done got gassed by the fact that we let this nigga off."

Reggie told Lil Red that Jake was his people and that Jake wasn't aware of their gang, he was only trying to get to the bottom of a death-threat letter he'd received. "He wasn't trying to play anyone," Reggie tried to assure them.

Being the diplomatic leader of the two, Dollar interrupted, "Your man just sent two of my top earners to the nurse leaving me with no one to collect my shit. How do you suppose we're going to fix that, Regg?" In the back of his mind Jake knew he should be quiet but there was something about the whole play that was bothering him deep in his heart. He was a cool, humble guy who didn't want any problems, but something in his brain clicked and told him there was a possibility he could do a lot of years and could be here for a while . . . and if that was the case then he couldn't tolerate shit like this from niggaz like Dollar, Lil Red, and even niggaz like his homie Reggie. So Jake spoke up.

"What would you have done if I killed them two faggots?"

The yard got silent, even Reggie was shocked by the outburst. But Jake didn't stop there. "You should act like they're dead anyway 'cause if I get in my house and they front again I'll kill both them faggots." Before Reggie could cut in, Jake thanked him for all he was trying to do and continued to berate the brothers, saying things like if they hadn't walked over with so many niggaz he would have fucked them up, too . . . and that both of them could get a fair one whenever they wanted. He turned to Reggie again. "I don't want you getting in the middle of this shit, it's my beef," then added, "plus them Northside niggaz pussy." As the words were being spit out his mouth, Northside dudes swarmed in on him.

Somebody yelled out, "Chill!" It was Dollar Bill that had spoken and his crew listened. He walked up to Jake with an extended hand and a smile. Jake left it hanging. "You got balls as big as an elephants," Dollar complimented. "I respect any man that has that much courage." Lil Red didn't take his brother's position too well, but he didn't want to disagree with Dollar in front of soldiers and outsiders. So he remained silent, and the Northside niggaz turned and walked away.

Reggie turned to his gung ho friend and said, "That wasn't the smartest move but it worked." Jake knew that it actually hadn't worked . . . the plan was to get one or both of the brothers to commit to a fair fight. He felt he was getting to Lil Red but it seemed Dollar was much too smart for his little ploy. *Odd that Dollar was the one that backed up,* he thought. With his tall and wide frame he appeared to be the physical one, but Jake would find out soon enough that it was really Lil Red who loved contact the most.

Rec time was over and the COs were yelling for them to get

off the yard. As Reggie and Jake walked back to the building, Reggie shared a few things with his friend to help keep him on point. He didn't like how he handled his business in the yard but what was done was done. "Keep your eyes open because Dollar is not one to be trusted, and Lil Red might be just plain old loose and stupid, but together they're a deadly team."

"I'm going to get bailed out in a few," Jake replied. "I can lay low until then, but seriously, you have your own shit going on. You don't need to get caught up in mine."

"Stopping tripping, nigga, that's the least I can do. I never forget a favor." When they were in high school, Jake held him down a couple of times when dudes wanted to give Reggie a beat down . . . and one time Jake actually stood up and fought a nigga for him. Reggie gave his old friend a dap. "Don't worry but be careful."

CHAPTER 4

MAN DOWN

Once again Jake was approached by CO Frazier when he got back to his dorm. Frazier's voice was more animated than when they had spoken earlier. "Are you fucking crazy?" he asked as if it was a legitimate question.

"Maybe," Jake said, "but I know I don't want you to move me."

"The only reason I'm not going to move you is because shit might get worse for you in another house. I heard you was willing to bang heads with the mighty Dollar and his brother Lil Red." Frazier shook his head. "Listen, I definitely got respect for you, Mr. Billings. I know you ain't the PC type, but be careful . . . very careful."

"Yeah, I got you," Jake said. On that note he strolled back to his bunk and was soon approached by a small white man.

"Billings, I have something for you."

Jake stared the little white man down before asking what.

"I never look in anything; I just deliver it," he said, handing Jake a newspaper. The paper was heavier than it should have been; something was inside. As Jake slowly opened the paper, two things fell out onto his lap: a knife and an envelope. Jake put the knife under his pillow for the moment, then he examined the outside of the envelope and opened it.

It read:

Dear J.B. today must have been a hell of a day for you. I guess that bitch gave you bad news on your visit. The little TV trick was nice and I give you credit on the way you handled the big niggaz. Also, that stunt you pulled in the yard was classic shit but it was stupid. Now you have beef with too many people for no reason but they won't get to you before I do, and I hope you're not trying to get help from your man downstairs 'cause ain't shit he can do for you. By the way I sent you a knife so you don't have to go around searching for one. I'm looking forward to taking you out later, hope you have some energy left because I'm going to carve you like a turkey!!!!

Truly yours,
Real Nigga, Same Dorm

This bullshit letter writing was getting on Jake's nerves but he couldn't let it show. He took a deep breath to regain his composure, and with a big smile on his face he got the knife from under his pillow and placed it nicely back in the newspaper along with the envelope and letter, then threw it all in the hallway garbage. *Okay, Mister Letter Writer, you got me out of character once but it won't happen again.*

Moments later a loud agonizing scream echoed off the walls of the block; it originated somewhere to Jake's left. He looked around to find the source of the scream, but he didn't see anything at first. Then there it was: The little white guy, who had not long ago delivered him the goods, was laying in a fetal position clutching what was left of his face. From the looks of the wounds someone had splashed him with some kind of boiling liquid; probably baby oil. It didn't look good for him at all—his face was melting in his hands. This left Jake feeling bad for two reasons: He felt genuinely sorry for how the little guy would look and feel after that day, and because he wouldn't be able to ask Melted Face who sent him any time soon.

This melting face incident put Jake in a whole different mind-frame—he was more anxious than normal, than ever before. He could tell by all the events that had happened that death was very much in the air. He started to think that maybe it was his turn to go. He had definitely done more than his share of dirt . . . The letter writer was right: What comes around goes around. Well, he would soon find out. Then the turtles came. Jake chuckled to himself because he knew how pissed off CO Fraze had to be about this one. There was definitely going to be some report writing and talking to the captain over some shit like this.

The turtles practically fucked the whole dorm up for nothing. Tossing inmates, flipping their bunks, and emptying their bins. All they had was a victim; there was no one to blame it on.

So they did the next best thing they figured they could do: searched for drugs and weapons. While they were doing that, any man who acted like they had a problem got fucked up in the process. Jake was glad he'd thrown that knife out; that was the last thing he needed to get caught with. That would have been another charge and Lord knows he didn't need that.

A CO yelled, "Oh yeah, we got 'em." The COs were standing by Ike's bunk with a big Ziploc bag filled with weed. From where Jake was it looked to be at least a quarter of a pound. Then he pulled out a smaller Ziploc filled with pills alongside about two ounces of base.

"I got one over here," another one of the armor-clad COs yelled. Now they were standing by Cory's bunk. This one pulled out ten bundles of heroin, what seemed to be about a hundred loose bags of dust, and a Rambo knife.

Looking at the knife Jake was glad they didn't try to use it on him, but he figured the only reason they hadn't brought it to the fight was because they assumed the two of them could pound him out without a weapon. They would have tried the knife later. Jake had a hunch: Being that Ike and Cory weren't there to stash their shit before the turtles came through—they were still in medical tending to their wounds—the Northside Boys were going to blame him for their losses. *Oh shit,* he said to himself as he ran down the day's events in his mind: the letter, bumping into Regg, Kim flipping on him during the visit, the fight in the dorm, the almost big showdown in the yard with the Northside Boys, the talks with CO Frazier, the delivery from the small white man, the small white man getting his shit burnt up, and the raid on the house. This shit can't be real. Jake knew he couldn't afford to go to sleep tonight because if he did that could very well be his last sleep. He decided to pull up a chair by the TV where he hoped no one would be bold enough to set it off because the CO in the bubble kept a constant watch on that area. He could get a couple of z's there—with one eye open of course. But before he did he was going to make a collect call that could solve all his problems.

Jake was owed a favor by a very powerful person or rather a person close to a powerful person. Her name was Mary-beth Jenkins. Her friends called her Legs and most of her clients called her M.B. Jake went to the phone and dialed the ten-digit number with the zero in front; he stated his name for the operator. Jake waited for the ring and the whole collect-call-from-a-correctional-facility song and dance, then he heard the voice he was waitng for.

"Hello, Jake. How are you? Long time no hear."

In a cool tone, as if he was under no stress, Jake replied back, "Cut the bullshit M.B. I need a favor from you and I need it fast." Then, "I need you to hire one of your clients for me and you know exactly who I'm talking about. Tell him I don't need him for the whole case, I just need him to represent me for a bail hearing. Once I'm out I will get someone else, but I don't have court for a few days and I'm caught up in some shit up in here that's life threatening." Not letting her get a word in till he finished, he continued, "Now I know for a fact you two might be reluctant to help me due to the circumstances, but let's not forget fair is fair."

"You're a cold son of a bitch," Mary-beth scolded. "I would have thought you knew me better than that by now. I know fair is fair and before you called I was already on top of the situation. If you would have gotten to know me better you wouldn't have had to approach me on that cold-as-ice shit like you do everybody else." Jake was relieved by what he heard. "There will be someone in the courthouse representing you tomorrow, and after your bail is set I'll make sure you get out. Is that okay with you Mr. Ice?"

"If you make this happen consider us even across the board, but please don't ever run that get-to-know-you-better shit on me again. The reason I come at you the way I do is because I know you. So don't think because we slept together, again, that I'm thinking with my dick and not my brain, a'ight." She barely got a chance to respond before Jake hung up and went back to his spot to catch some one-eye-open z's.

Jake had met Mary-beth one day while he was trying to do some shopping for Kim. He did a lot of things that day that were totally out of his character. For starters he took five gees out of his stash and decided to go to Mitch's gambling spot. He wasn't a real risk taker usually but ended up leaving with twenty-two gees. He took his seventeen gees profit to Neiman Marcus and walked straight to the women's section—he was having one of his soft moments. Being that he had on his hood uniform—Carhartt hoody, hard blue denim jeans, and his Chukkas—none of the salespeople were fucking with him. They probably thought he was coming to steal or just window-shop. Not really knowing what he wanted, Jake starting surveying the room. He looked to his left: nothing, then to his right: still nothing, then he turned and looked behind him and spotted what he was looking for—a dime piece with a freshly did hairdo. She had a pretty brown complexion, not short but not too tall, fully dipped in the flyest gear: nice bag, nice shoes, and if he had to bet she was probably driving a pretty little coupe like a C-Class or 3 Series Beamer or something.

Jake decided to approach her and get straight to the point. "Um, excuse me, miss, are you with someone?"

"Why?" she asked.

Jake liked her spunk. "Because I would like to ask for some help if you're not," he told her.

"Is that always how you come on to women? With the you-need-help line?"

Jake laughed. "Nah, I usually just say 'What up, ma? You look good—what's your math?' "

"Does that work?" she asked.

"Eighty percent of the time," he admitted before adding, "Besides, I didn't say I needed your help, I said I was going to ask for it." When she asked him his name he said: "J.B., what's yours?"

When she answered "M.B.," they both shared a small laugh. M.B. interrupted the jovial moment with, "What do you need help with?"

"Well," he said, "being that you so stylish and well put together I was going to ask your advice on the latest women's shoes and bags. You know, put a brotha up on what's popping! I need to know what the women want these days."

"Stick with Chanel or Lou V.; you can't lose with those." Then she smiled and said, "I'll show you a pair of shoes and a bag practically every woman would nearly die over." She showed him a nice Lou bag that cost twenty-five hundred and some Chanel shoes that ran twelve hundred.

Jake liked the two pieces that she'd showed him and knew that Kim would, too. He was holding the bag in his hand when he said, "One more thing, ma."

"You want my number," she said with a straight face.

"Well, actually I was going to ask you to show me a good bottle of perfume." She suggested a bottle of CREED. He walked over to the perfume counter, got the big gold bottle of CREED that ran about five hundred and some change, then gave it to Mary-beth after he purchased it.

Mary-beth said it was sweet of him to buy the perfume but he didn't have to—he was cool and it was her pleasure to help him. "And I didn't mean to sound ungrateful." She could feel a connection to this guy; he made her feel comfortable—comfortable enough to ask if he knew where she could get some good weed from.

Jake gave a light chuckle. "What, are you police?"

She paused for a second. The look on her face had Jake believing she was keeping it one hundred with him.

"Let me find out somebody like you smokes."

"You'd be surprised what a girl like me does."

He liked that. "Yeah, well, I can take care of that for you, how much you need? I got a few bags in the car." She said "Cool," and after Jake bought the bag and shoes, they both headed toward the parking lot.

Both of them chose to stay quiet as they walked toward the car. It was silent but it wasn't uncomfortable—both of them thinking how interesting the other was. Jake stopped at a brand-new Cadillac truck. It was nice; nothing special about it. He opened the passenger's-side back door and hopped in. The driver said, "Damn, that was quick," and raised the back of the driver's seat out of its reclining position. "I barely shut my eyes," he added.

"Sleep when your dead, homie, we got moves to make," Jake told his friend Nine-One. Nine-One was Jake's favorite driver. He always held him down and put him before all his other customers. Jake reached into a bag in the back, grabbed two dubs, and handed them to Mary-beth. Then he wrote his number on a piece of paper and told her to hit him up if she want some more—that's all he had on him right now.

She thanked him and said it was a pleasure to meet him and she definitely would give him a call.

———

Just as Jake was reminiscing, something told him to be alert. When he looked, two dudes were approaching him. He guessed they could read his body language because one of them said, "Nah, gee, it ain't like that, we T.M.B." One said his name was Clips and the other said his name was Frankie. "Regg is our peoples," the one called Clips said. "He told us to hold you down, fam."

"That's good looking," Jake told the two men, "but I told Regg I was a'ight."

Frankie said, "I hear you, fam, and I seen you scrap so I know you can hold it down, but this is a nasty house and them boys you fucked up don't play fair. There're going to be a lot more niggaz coming for you, we just here to make sure it's an even fight, you know."

Clips added, "Regg said you was a stand-up thoroughbred kinda nigga, but even a thoroughbred can get on the wrong track. We just here to make sure if you need a banga you get a banga. Before lights out let a nigga know if you need something to eat or whatever, homie. We respect that work you put in and the way you carried yourself in the yard. It's been a long time since I seen a nigga man up to that many niggaz and be ready to get it in."

Frankie nodded his head. "Yeah, that was some real brave-heart shit, my nigga." And he gave Jake a dap.

Jake was thinking that the smart thing to do was to be humble and ask one of them to watch his back for a few while he caught some z's. But what if they were the ones who wanted to kill him? He would be finished real quick. Damned if he did, damned if he didn't; what was he to do? And before he could come up with any kind of answer, he felt something hot going into his back.

Frankie slid a six-and-a-half-inch blade into him. He had been hit real decent from the back and Jake knew it. How could he let this happen? Clips tried to catch him in the face, but unlike the first blow, Jake saw this one coming and put his hand up just in time to get it in his palm instead of his face. Jake was pulsing with adrenaline, enabling him to kick Clips in the ribs and nuts. But despite his efforts, he got hit twice more in the back by Frankie. Jake felt his legs go out from under him, and he fell to the floor. That didn't stop the two killers from getting their thing off. They started stomping him out, leaving Jake broken and bloody. Then Frankie put on the finishing touch: stabbing Jake in the top of his head with one of the razor-sharp blades.

That was all Jake's body could take. He saw a blinding white light all around, then nothing.

CHAPTER 5

GANGSTAS RIDE

Reggie flipped out when the news about the attack on his friend reached his dorm. Word had spread through the jail that the hit was brutal even for jail standards, and Reggie felt even worse after hearing that the niggaz that did it used his name to get close enough to make Jake relax his guard. Reggie knew both Frankie and Clips, and neither one of them was down with the Northside Boys. He couldn't figure out why they did what they did to Jake or how they had the balls to use his name, but he sure was going to find out on the way to nighttime rec.

Reggie had no idea what he was in store for at rec call, nor were any of the COs prepared for what was about to go down. The Northside Boys had decided to fold their hands, bowing down to the mysterious 300 Crew. Some people said there were only ten members in the jail, others thought there had to be three hundred of them running all the worldly goods in and out of the facility. Whoever they were, the 300 Crew supplied sneakers, knives, cellphones, porn mags, whatever you needed. Nobody ever fucked them over because instead of hurting you, they would use their outside connects to get to a family member or a significant other. It was said that each member was capable of killing a man with his bare hands and over the past ten years they averaged three hundred bodies a year, which led to them being named the 300 Crew. No one knew who they where. They had allegedly each gotten a life sentence for murder, extortion, or kidnapping and not one of them snitched. Some say they are stronger now that they are locked down and are making more than a hundred thousand dollars a week. The shit sounded far-fetched and unbelievable.

As soon as Reggie got to the yard he was approached by Lil Red and Dollar. Red started off the convo. "Yeah, nigga, look like ya man headed to heaven or hell. Heard they had to bring him outta there on a stretcher."

"So y'all niggaz is hiring mu'fuckaz to put your work in for you now? And y'all had them niggaz get close off the strength of my name," Reggie accused. "I guess y'all niggaz is pussy after all. Both y'all cowards can suck my dick, and I would gladly see any of you two faggots in the bathroom—hands, knife fight, whatever—but one of y'all niggaz got to see me."

Lil Red got real hype. "You and I can play the bathroom right now, Regg. I'll murder yo bitch ass. You ain't hard motherfucka."

Dollar hopped in, told his brother to chill, then said to Regg, "It's like this, homie, that shit that happened today wasn't personal, it was business. I know that's your homeboy but he fucked up a lot of money that belonged to us." Dollar went on to explain, "If he hadn't pulled that stunt earlier in the house, Ike and Cory wouldn't have said shit to him. There wouldn't of been no fight, none of that tough-guy shit in the yard earlier. My boys would have been on point and we wouldn't have lost all that money when the turtles flipped the house. Besides that he had it coming to him for trying to be the hardest nigga in the world! And that's not the only reason I'm approaching you. I came to give you a heads-up." After being sure he had Reggie's attention, Dollar continued, "The North-side Boys and the Spanish Crowns are both going to attack T.M.B. Both gangs are putting a lot of work in for the 300 Crew and getting paid well for it. You guys are in the way all the time so either you get down or lay down. It's a lot of cash to be made so I suggest you think about it very carefully."

"Ain't nothing to think about," Reggie said. "Hell no, T.M.B is T.M.B. and we ain't getting down with nobody. If you and the Crowns decide to set it, be my guest. Matter of fact," he added, "let's get it in right now." Reggie punctuated his statement by running straight at Lil Red and Dollar, but what Regg didn't know was that the 300 had got at more than half of his crew and paid them off to fall back. That left Reggie left to set it with only about ten or twelve soldiers to scrap with him. They didn't have a chance, but all of T.M.B. that didn't take the pay went out like the warriors they were. Regg never made it to Lil Red or Dollar. Instead he was swarmed by a bunch of Northside and Spanish Crown soldiers. None of the members of T.M.B. got done like they did Jake but they all received official beat-downs. They had to take solace in the fact that at least there weren't any murders; they would all live to fight another day. The turtle squad came and shut the mini riot down, but the word was spread all over the jail that the takeover was official: The 300 Crew was running everything. As the turtles were bringing out all of the participants in plastic wire cuffs en route to the hole, all Regg could think about was how pussy the Northside, the Crowns, and T.M.B. members that sold out were. What kind of crew would work for another crew? He wondered how much money the 300 offered them, and why.

Reggie would get his answers soon enough, and he swore to get revenge on all T.M.B. niggaz who sold him out, which was most of them. But the last thing he thought about before falling to sleep in his cell was, *I wonder how J.B. doing.*

CHAPTER 6

AWAKE

Hospital room, January 2010

"Hey good-lookin', what's cooking?" Nurse Brenda Knight said in a tone that sounded as if she was about to sing. She wasn't looking at him when she said it; it was just what she always said to him when she entered his room for the first time that day. She had a special little thing she would say to all her patients. The lady who shared the room with Jake would have gotten a "Heeey, Boo-Boo, how are you?" if Jake hadn't scared the life out of her when he replied.

"I don't know but I'm hungry as hell," he whispered in a groggy voice that resembled the voice of the Godfather on his deathbed. Jake was even surprised by the way his voice sounded. It felt like his chest was caving in when he tried to clear his throat. His senses kicked into overdrive; his nose knew that hospital scent all too well and his eyes focused in on the young lady who had asked him the question.

"Oh my God," Nurse Knight exclaimed. She poured some water in his cup and raised it to Jake's mouth. After he got a few sips down the nurse ran out of the room saying something about being back in a second with a doctor and some other mumbo jumbo about Jesus and a few other things Jake couldn't quite make out.

Jake had no idea what the fuck was wrong with him or why he was in this hospital room. The last time he had awoken in a hospital was after a surgery on his tonsils, but something told him this was different and much more serious. He tried to move his extremities and quickly realized that his body was weak. His left hand felt numb, and he couldn't move his legs. Jake did manage to move his right hand and discovered how thin his arms, hands, and body felt to the touch. Then he reached up and felt his face. He had a beard that felt like a bush. He touched his head, which was full of hair—far from the baldy he loved to keep clean. He wondered what the fuck had happened to him. When the pretty nurse came back in with a doctor, Jake immediately shot his questions at the doctor, wanting to find out what was wrong with him and what had happened to him.

"Calm down, Mr. Billings," the doctor told him. "I'm Dr. Jenson, and you have been in a coma for about two years."

Jake couldn't remember anything, and the story about the coma sounded kind of suspect to him. "Okay, Doc, how did I manage to get into this coma you say I've been in?" Jake questioned.

The doctor removed a clipboard from the end of the bed and read through a few pages near the beginning of the thick binder. "Well, Mr. Billings, I've not always been your doctor, but according to your records, you were stabbed and beaten into a coma while you were incarcerated."

Still not really believing anything the doctor was saying, Jake asked, "I feel so weak, will I be okay?"

After Dr. Jenson gave Jake a thorough examination, he reported his findings. "Your left hand will never regain feeling, but everything else seems to be fine considering you haven't moved a muscle in two years. You are going to have to go to rehab to get the rest of your body moving again, but I think the prognosis is very favorable."

Jake thought about all Dr. Jenson had told him and asked, "How come I don't remember anything about the injury?"

"It's fairly common for a patient not to remember certain things after awakening from a long coma. Sometimes the brain blocks out certain things for reasons of its own."

"Will I get my memory back, Doctor?"

"I can't say for certain that you will, but I can tell you that a great deal of patients who suffer memory loss like yours do get it back."

Who the hell could put me in a coma? What was I in jail for? Do I have to go back? Is the case opened or closed? All these thoughts raced through his head.

Nurse Knight spoke to him in a soft voice. "I know you have a lot of questions you want answered, and in due time they will be. But for now," she said, "you should really try to get some rest. You will be filled in on everything later." The nurse felt bad for Jake. There was a lot to digest after waking up from a two-year sleep, but he should be thanking the good Lord. *Not many people get a second chance,* Brenda thought.

Brenda was a twenty-eight-year-old lady who had been a nurse for seven years. She felt being a nurse was one of the best jobs in the world, second only to being a doctor, which she would have been if she had the money for medical school. Since she didn't, she grinded extra hard and prayed that the good Lord would see fit for her to make enough money to pay for college. She would start in about a year and a half, if everything worked out. It wasn't looking so good, though, with her mom being sick and her nine-year-old boy having Attention Deficit Disorder, but Brenda believed the man upstairs could fix all things big and small. After all, He'd already delivered a stand-up guy into her life.

CHAPTER 7

PLOTS AND PLANS

January 2008

Mary-beth Jenkins and Phillip Rosenberg were sitting in the back of his 760 BMW. Mary-beth and Phil had been business partners and lovers for so many years that Phil felt there was hardly a line between the two. Mary-beth, on the other hand, understood the boundaries. Phil was 5'11", and while his face and body looked like a young Richard Grieco's, his attitude and swagger were more like Donald Trump's.

"Did you take care of the J.B. situation today?"

"Yes, honey, he should be on the way out as we speak." Phil let the lie fly off his tongue as if it was the truth.

Franklin Butler was being held in the county jail for attempted murder and kidnapping. Frank's case wasn't run-of-the-mill. He was a fifth-degree black belt and taught the art at the local dojo alongside his brother Mike. Frank taught on Mondays, Wednesdays, and Fridays. Mike took over on Tuesdays, Thursdays, and Saturdays. It was Frank's day off, and he decided to go say what's up to his brother and hang out with him. It had been awhile since they'd just sat around and kicked it with each other. All of the students were gone, and Frank had a forty-dollar-bottle of Hennessy in hand. It had been at least two years since the brothers had shared a bottle of cognac. If Frank wasn't married to the ultimate stank bitch who kept tabs all the time, he would have invited Mike to go out to a club with him like they used to, but that was definitely out of the question with Laura always threatening to divorce him over any little thing that pissed her off.

When Frank got to the door, what he heard made his knees buckle. He would have known that female moan anywhere. Then there was his brother's voice.

"Do you like this dick?"—in between deep breaths—"Tell me how much you like this dick."

Frank opened the door as quietly as he could and walked up the stairs of the dojo. When he made it to the top, there they were: Mike had his wife Laura bent over doggy-style.

As Frank tiptoed toward them, Laura must have heard a squeak from one of the floorboards. She looked toward the noise and Mike followed her lead, but it was too late. Frank's leg was already in the air and it came smashing down on his brother's back. A cracking sound and Mike's scream let Frank know his brother would most likely be crippled for life. Mike and Laura were stuck together like two dogs in heat, but Frank wasn't finished yet. He pulled his brother off his wife and threw him out the window all in one motion. Next, without even thinking about what he was doing, Frank chopped his wife across the throat. Laura collapsed to the floor. Then he took a handful of her hair and dragged her unconscious body down both flights of steps, out the dojo, and to his car. He stood her up and punched her in the face so hard she awakened, and then he hit her again to put her back to sleep. He threw her in the car and walked over to his brother who was laid out on his stomach with a split forehead and plenty of broken bones.

Frank turned him over on his back and grabbed Mike by both feet. What he did next was unthinkable. He spread his brother's legs apart and proceeded to stomp his dick and balls with five of the hardest stomps he could deliver. Unfazed by the damage he'd caused, Frank left his brother lying there, not knowing or caring if he was dead or alive, and walked back to his car. He climbed into the front seat of his Ford and said to his wife, "This is going to be the last ride we ever take together." Luckily for her, he only made it four blocks before the cops pulled him over. Somebody in a passing car had seen his brother flying out the window and called the cops.

When Frank called Phil to represent him, Phil thought he could beat the kidnapping charge—that was a bullshit charge—but the attempted murder was a different story altogether. Even if Phil could manage to win it all, he knew there was no way Frank would be able to raise enough money to pay him to do so. The fact that Phil had gone to school with Frank and played pick-up basketball with him on Tuesdays didn't amount to jack shit in Phil's eyes. Phil thought about taking the case pro bono but after giving it a second thought, he had to be paid, and not getting paid was not in his character. He held off on responding, keeping Frank anxious for damn near a week.

When Frank was called down for a lawyer's visit and saw that it was Phil, his face lit up. It was the first time he felt like things may be all right since the night of the incident. Phil cut straight to the chase. "Frank, you don't have the money to beat this case and if you don't have a lawyer on a case like this you lose everything. The least amount of years you're looking at is twenty, and that's if you're lucky, but I'm here today to help you out. If you do me a favor . . . I'll do a favor for you. Get my drift?"

Frank nodded his head. He had a feeling, though, that whatever it was Phil had in mind was going to probably get him into even more shit but he had no choice.

Phil looked around before scribbling three words on the notepad he had in front of him.

TAKE HIM OUT

Then he lifted the page and there was a picture of Jake. Phil ripped up the note paper with the message and looked directly into Frank's eyes. "Do you know this man?"

"I've seen 'im."

"If you can do that for me," Phil said, "I can get you off scot-free. I promise! The judge and DA you'll be in front of are close friends of mine."

Frank thought about the proposition. He knew that Phil was a grimy bitch. He could have helped him without making him commit another crime. *I went to school with this cracker,* he thought. *I play ball with him yet he wants me to take a nigga out for him before he'll give me any help.* He imagined getting out and following Phil home after a game and snapping his fucking neck. Then he said, "Yeah, I can make that happen, Phil."

"Then you got yourself a lawyer," Phil said.

When it was all said and done, Frank felt this was his lucky day because Phil had shown him a picture of a dude that was in the same house as he was. Frank had watched the man handle two big dudes from the Northside clique with ease. Then he watched him go to the yard and kick it with that kid Regg from T.M.B. After that, the kid was ready to go head up with the leaders of the Northside. It was easy for Frank to figure out a quick little plan—just go to the Northside Boys and offer his services to take out Jake. Frank felt a little bad that he was going to have to take someone out, but if that was what he had to do to be a free man again, so be it.

Frank went back upstairs to where he was housed and called his man Clips to his bunk. "Yo, let me do your job and bring the book cart to all the houses, I got to holla at somebody upstairs for something," he said.

Clips replied, "Cool, my nigga, I was tired anyway. I'll just tell the CO in the bubble that I'm sick and you're gonna do the job for me."

Frankie delivered the books to all the houses as promised, and when he got to where Lil Red and Dollar were bunked he offered to take Jake out for them . . . for a light fee.

Lil Red asked Frank, "What the fuck makes you think we need your help?"

Frank answered him very bluntly. "Because I can kill with my bare hands and the two hardest dudes you had in the house already got fucked up. Besides, after your little altercation in the yard, if anything happened to the dude during rec, you two would be the prime suspects. I'm offering my services for a small fee: some weed, tobacco, two pairs of kicks, and one of them ho CO bitches y'all got under your thumb."

Dollar sort of liked the idea of having somebody take care of the business who wasn't affiliated with them in any way. "What makes you think you can handle him?" he asked.

"Because I'm a black belt in three different martial arts, I own my own dojo, and I have a plan." Frank went on to explain. "I'm gonna approach him with a friend like we're down with T.M.B., being that he and that kid Regg are homies. We'll make him think that we're there to hold him down, and when we rock him to sleep I'm gonna finish him."

Dollar liked the idea but it had a little flaw. "What about the real T.M.B. members that's in the house?"

Frank answered him honestly. "I had planned on crossing that road when I got to it, but I had an idea I was going to knock out the real T.M.B. cats, sit them on the stall until it was over."

Dollar chuckled to himself. He admired Frank's audacity but said, "That won't be necessary. Their loyalty to their clique has already been compromised. No one will jump in. You got the job. If you succeed there's a lot more in it for you than what you asked for. You could actually get a great position in this new clique we're forming."

Frank didn't give a fuck about any clique. In fact he didn't care about the kicks and shit, he only asked for those things because he wanted Clips's help. He knew Clips had a bid to do and didn't have any support from the outside. All he wanted was to get out of this stinking-ass jail, but he said, "Yeah, that's cool."

Lil Red spoke up. "I have one request in the way I want the business handled."

Frank gave Lil Red his attention. "What's the request?"

"I want him stabbed in the head; can you do that?"

Frank said "Yeah" quickly and wished to himself he could stab this prick Lil Red in the head, then he asked Dollar, "How you know T.M.B. members won't jump in for sure?"

"Because after tonight there will be no more Northside, no more T.M.B., no more Crowns, just the 300 Crew. And whoever don't want to be down with that dies!"

Frank had heard of Lil Red and Dollar on the streets. The Northside was supposed to be live—all those crews were. He struggled to understand how any of them could fold their hands so easily. Maybe the 300 had offered a lot of money to put all of these crews together and had some kind of plan to take over the whole city. Frank got some of the answers to his questions from Dollar.

"This gang shit is for the birds," Dollar said. "Now is the time to organize and I have plans. Especially since me and my brother's time is up in two years. I'm a well-connected man, and so are some of the Crowns. Same for some of T.M.B. Why not get together and take over everything? Why not be one big family?" He mused over his own question before going on. "I'll tell you why: It's because of a bunch of egos. Fuck that, I need millions and whoever can't understand that is in the way and needs to be taken out." Dollar put his hand on Frank's shoulder. "That's why I'm giving you the job, and when you're done I'll make sure you get everything you asked for and then some, but if you happen to fuck up that's on you. You mention me or anyone else's name—"

"You're dead." Lil Red hopped into the conversation, "Karate or not. So make sure you do that shit right!"

Frank remained humble. From the skills he'd developed through all his years of training, he knew he could have killed these two clowns in less than a minute for speaking disrespectful to him, but he calmly said, "Cool, the job will get done and done correct. I won't need anything else from you guys except the payment that I asked for." Frank thought he would hate to be in Jake's position with so many people wanting him dead, especially when it was dudes like gang members and lawyers. "Since you want him stabbed in the head," Frank was talking directly to Lil Red, "you should make sure you get me two knives and six pair of kitchen gloves."

"Cool, ninja man, I like your style," Lil Red said with a smile.

After the conversation with the two brothers, Frank pushed the cart back to his assigned house in the jail and called his man Clips to his bunk.

Frank and Clips had recently become friends. Clips pulled Frank's coat as to who was who as far as the gang members. He also assured Frank that he was with no gang and thought that most of the dudes in them was pussy; they were fronting due to their affiliation. "As a matter of fact," Clips told Frank, "I would love to hurt one of them faggots if I had an opportunity." From that day on Frank and Clips remained cool and hung with each other tough. Frank could tell Clips was a loose cannon and had a lot of anger in him, but he admired his point of view.

"When it comes to being locked up," Clips told Frank one day, "sometimes I wake up happy that I'm locked up because if I was free someone would probably be getting killed right now." Then he laughed to himself and stared into space for about ten seconds before asking, "You know what I mean, bro?"

Clips never told Frank what he was in for, but he didn't have to; Frank knew it was murder. He knew by the look in his eyes what Clips was capable of. As a teacher of martial arts he could tell when someone was on the edge. But Clips was real cool about everything, cool enough that Frank wanted to make sure he sent the brother a package as often as he could after Phil got him out of there. He snapped back, got focused, and asked Clips, "You ready to get paid and live it up for a minute?"

"I ain't got shit better to do," Clips said. "Let's get it on, baby."

Frank told him what he wanted to do and about the conversation he had with Red and Dollar. Of course he left out the real reason he was doing the hit. He hated using Clips without being fully straight with him but that was the way it had to be.

This type of action was right up Clips's alley. This is what he dreamed about when he laid down in his bunk at night. He asked Frank, "Can we keep this shit going after this?"

"Maybe," Frank said, "but here's how we're going to do it." He laid the plan down. "Ain't nobody tellin' nothing. Everything should run real smooth."

Clips was crazy with excitement.

Frank asked him once more, "Now, you sure you want to do this? You don't have to. When I collect I'm going to still hit you off anyway. You been holding me down since I got here and I appreciate that."

"Fuck you talkin' about?" Clips asked. "You know I'm wit' you one hundred percent. Besides, I'm going to be locked up for the rest of my life; I ain't never going home. If you ride out, I ride out, nigga. It is what it is."

With that being said, the plan was in full effect.

CHAPTER 8

MITCH AND MONSTER

January 2010

"J.B. is more official than niggaz' whole team. Niggaz said he was in a coma and all that but I'm telling you that nigga was fronting, he did that shit to beat that case. Dude's a live-ass nigga and I bet a gee-stack that friends and family members connected to the motherfuckers who touched him start dropping like flies," said Mitch to Monster.

Mitch was forty-four years old and drove a classic '96 Cadillac Eldorado that looked like it just came from the dealer or the candy-paint shop. He ran numbers and owned the neighborhood gambling spot, and could always be found in the spot even though he only lived a few blocks away. His man, Monster, was twenty years younger than Mitch and housed all the dice games at the spot. He kept track of all the bets—and on the niggaz making them. Monster was like Mitch's little brother and was also his muscle, and as far as niggaz in the hood were concerned, he was the closest thing to Bruce Lee.

"Hell no," Monster shot back. "I know a nigga who was in there when that shit jumped off. He said J.B. went out like a trooper but them niggaz put that work in on him. The nigga that put me up on the bizness even saluted the nigga for being alive. Said that nine out of ten niggaz would have died on the spot. And besides that my Old Gee, that little hood-rat bitch Tanya that you bangin', is J.B.'s ole girlfriend's cuzzin. And Tanya told me that Kim is fucked up over that shit because she left that nigga for dead when he was in the joint. She said Kim went to see the nigga in the hospital and came home broken down, crying. Talking 'bout the nigga only weighs a hundred pounds, he got a beard like a castaway or Jesus or some shit like that. So your man ain't frontin', that nigga is finished."

"That's what's wrong with y'all young niggaz nowadays," Mitch said. "You don't know the difference between a class act and a class clown."

"What do you mean by that?"

"What I mean, my man, is that everything you told me I already knew. First of all, when you spoke on that hood-rat Tanya that I'm hitting, you should have said 'that *we* hitting.' But you want to try to cuff the bitch or act like you ain't digging her out, too, when she ain't shit but a jump-off. Then you come in here with that weak-ass pillow talk she gave you like she only talk for you. Keep believing everything a ho say! And as far as the nigga who said he was there: Fuck that nosy, spreading-the-word-ass nigga. I bet he never put no work in not one day in his measly life."

Monster knew better than to piss Mitch off because even though he was Mitch's muscle, he was also Mitch's student. He learned everything he knew from Mitch: fighting, hustling, gaming, women all the way down to dressing and talking edu-cated when he was around certain kinds of people. Not to men-tion the last three niggaz who tried Mitch had all ended up in a pine box. Funny thing about it was that Mitch was conveniently out of town when all of the victims found their demise. Even though they never spoke on the situation, Monster knew Mitch was responsible for their deaths.

Monster, using his head, apologized to Mitch about the bitch. "Come on, Mitch. Let's go get some liquor and weed, that hood-rat Tanya, and one of her dingy-ass friends and have a good time."

Mitch wasn't the type to get too hype over most shit and he felt a little funny about flipping on Monster, so like the gee he was, he returned the apology to his man. But he thought, *I hope one day I ain't got to take this outta town trip on my nigga.* And at the very same time Monster was thinking: *I might have to take this nigga down one day. He may be my teacher, but he ain't as strong as I am.*

Mitch and Monster were sitting in the spot masking their thoughts with alcohol and weed while they waited on Tanya and her friend to show up when somebody banged on the door.

The knocking was replaced with a yell. "Yo, Monster, you in there?"

Everybody in the hood knew that the spot didn't open until it was dark and they also knew better than to be screaming on Mitch's block. *Whoever was at the door was stupid and about to get their ass kicked,* Monster thought as he walked toward the door.

Mitch got a bad vibe. "Don't open it!" he said, but Monster already had his hand on the doorknob when the first shot rang through the door.

The shot missed Monster's face by a few inches, but he lost his footing and fell backward. Monster's .40 cal. was off his waist and sparking off before his backside ever made impact with the floor. He spit three slugs from the huge handgun back in the direction of the door. No more shots came from the outside, so Monster figured whoever it was must have run when they heard the shots, or someone was dead on the other side of the door.

Mitch and Monster checked outside and saw nothing. No bodies. No blood. No nothing. They had no idea who had tried to take them out, or at least Monster didn't. As for Mitch, that was a different ball game altogether. He could and would find out later when he watched the footage from the hidden cameras he had strategically stashed in and around the building. And when he did, he would surely be taking a vacation, and whoever had been on the other side of the door would surely be taking a long dirt nap.

Monster knew that with all the money flowing around the spot, and all the jealous motherfuckers in the hood, it could have been anyone. He had a funny feeling that they would be back, and he was right—but he didn't know how right he was. Monster and Mitch were still outside when two men came tearing around the corner in a blue hoopty. Monster thought, *These clowns must be crazy,* and they were.

The two dust-heads was from around the way. They'd lost their re-up money at the dice table with Monster two days ago and wanted it back. Monster saw the hoopty spin around the corner first, and before he could yell to Mitch to watch out, he heard:

BOOM! BOOM! BOOM! BOOM!

Mitch was letting off a big, government-issued Colt .45 bulldog. Two of the slugs from the weapon caught the driver, causing the car he was driving to hit another before flipping over three times. Mitch took off running toward the wrecked car while it was still tumbling, letting off three more shots, killing both men. It had been a long time since Mitch had actually murdered someone himself, and it made him excited to the point where his dick was hard. His adrenaline was high and he wanted to kill someone else. He would have pumped more shots into the already dead bodies but he only had seven hollow points in the clip. After Monster caught up, he said, "Come on, Mitch, we gotta get out of here." Mitch took heed to his friend's warning. They ran in the spot to lock it up and then ran out the back door and into Monster's hoopty.

They headed downtown to get some drinks and throw the Colt .45 into the river. People from around their way tended to mind their business and they definitely knew better than to take the stand on a motherfucker, so Mitch wasn't really worried about any witnesses. Besides, the whole neighborhood was getting fed up with the dust-head stick-up kids anyway. A lot was running through Mitch's mind, but the thought that kept returning was: *Damn it felt good to kill again.* It made him reminisce over the days when he used to run the streets with a young teenage sidekick who was a certified murderer, a hell of a hustler, and the best nephew an uncle could ask for. His name was Jake Billings.

CHAPTER 9

CHEATING DEATH

Nurse Knight walked into Jake's room with a tray filled with fruits and juices. She expected to find a hungry man ravenous for food and answers to his many questions. But what she found took her totally by surprise: an empty bed. He must be in the washroom. She made a mental note to tell him how important it was for him to take it easy for a little longer. Brenda put the tray down and knocked on the washroom door, "Mr. Billings?"

No answer.

She knocked a little harder and tried calling him again. "Mr. Billings?" Now she was alarmed. What's going on? There was no way he had the strength in his legs, or any part of his body for that matter, to walk out of the hospital on his own. She hurried out of the room to the nurses' station and asked the duty nurse working the desk what happened to Mr. Billings. *Maybe he was taken for some tests,* Brenda thought, *that I wasn't aware of.*

"What do you mean what happened to him? He should be in his room," the duty nurse answered.

Brenda was dumbfounded. She pulled out her cellphone and called the doctor. The phone had rung twice when she heard his voice, "What can I do for you, Nurse Knight?" But the voice didn't come through the receiver of the phone. Brenda spun around and found the doctor behind her with his Black-Berry in his hand.

"Whew, you startled me," she said.

"You have to cut back on the morning coffee," he joked.

Ignoring his weak attempt at humor, she said, "I wanted to ask you who came and checked Mr. Billings out?"

"No one," the doctor said. "Not by my orders anyway. The man can barely move."

"He's gone," Brenda blurted. They both rushed over to the security booth and asked the cop on duty if he saw anyone leave with Mr. Billings.

The cop answered, "No, but I just came on. Let me call Ted; he worked the last shift." He made the phone call but got the same answer. The nurses called the nurses from the prior shift and posed the question to them. They all said they hadn't seen Mr. Billings outside of his room. This was the strangest thing that had happened in the hospital since two babies got switched about eight years ago. It was an official mystery: a man wakes up from a coma and disappears.

Brenda thought for a moment. "Aren't there surveillance cameras on this floor?" she asked.

"Sure," the cop said, "they're on all the floors. Follow me." Brenda and the doctor trailed the cop to a small room containing the machine that received digital feeds from all of the cameras. They fast-forwarded through the twenty-four hours of footage recorded on his floor and found nothing. After reviewing the feeds they knew no more than they knew before. Jake had no visitors, and the only people to come in and out of his room were the cafeteria people, the doctor, and Brenda.

Everyone was totally baffled. How can a man vanish into thin air? Then the cop shouted out, "I got it. I think I know how he did it." Brenda and the doctor both looked at the officer like, *Then spill it, Sherlock.* "He must have somehow gotten in the cafeteria cart and got rolled out," the cop proudly stated. It made sense; more sense than anything thus far.

That was until a little old Latina lady in the back shot that idea down quick with a "Nooo waaayyy, officer. I work food carts over twenty years." Then she went on to further explain why. "One: He can't fit under cart; too much food with big thermos. Two: I looking at the man when I give food. Then I turn 'round and leave the room and say bye. He was there when I say bye." That put the cop back at square one.

"Maybe he went through the ceiling in the bathroom," the cop said, shooting random thoughts out loud.

"It sounds like the only logical explanation," the doctor semi-agreed, "but it's nearly impossible with his medical condition. He's fresh off a coma, his legs barely work, and he has a bad arm. I can't see it," the doctor second-guessed himself.

"You must not have seen those Adidas commercials," a young, sassy NA said, adding her two cents. "Impossible is nothing. Kevin Garnett is my baby." Most everyone laughed at the girl's comment, but Brenda was at a loss for humor right now. Something about the whole ordeal was sending chills up and down her spine. She never lost anything . . . not her keys . . . not even that five pounds to fit back into her favorite jeans. This was way too eerie. Then, all she could think of was: What a God!

———

Meanwhile, Jake was thinking the same thing—*what a God*—but he also knew that there was a devil, and he had it on his back to prove it. There would be a lot more evil to deal with before this whole situation was over and done with. He turned his head left to face the driver and said, "Thanks for coming to help me, Kim. Somebody might have found out I woke up and come to finish me off."

Kim was trying to keep her composure. She couldn't believe that he was actually out of the coma. He had lost a lot of weight and grown a lot of hair, but here he was. "You don't look so good, babe, let me take you to another hospital somewhere else."

"I can't take that chance—the police might be looking for me."

"Looking for you for what?" Kim wanted to know.

Jake answered as honestly as he could, "I don't know. All of my memory of that jail shit hasn't come back to me yet. I can't remember what happened to me, not even what I was in jail for."

"Well you couldn't have committed a crime while you were asleep, so you should be fine," Kim said with a smile.

Other people knowing what he should know was starting to get to Jake a little. "Tell me what you know," he half asked and half demanded. "What was I locked up for?"

"Attempted murder," she calmly answered, and then went on to explain to Jake how some dudes tried to rob him in their store—*my* store, he swore she said—and he shot them. She ended the story by telling him that because he was harmed while in the care of the state, the DA showed mercy and exonerated him of all charges. "You're a free man, J.B. You ain't got nothing to worry about. You're safe."

Jake's intuition told him that although he may have been cut loose from the charges, he wasn't safe. He needed to know who put him in that coma and why. Then he had to return the favor to the person or people responsible. Whoever did it should have killed him, and if they had any idea who they were fucking with they would have. "How were we?" he asked Kim. "I mean . . . were we on good terms before all of this?"

Kim answered honestly, "No, but I think we should talk about that at another time. What's important is that you're alive"—and she meant that. "But I would like for you to tell me something."

"What?"

"How did you get out of that hospital in such a weak state?"

Jake looked her in the eyes and gave her an easy smile. "Easy," he said, "I knew what time the nurse would come check on me so I was hiding behind the door, which is left open at all times. When she ran out the room after not seeing me in the bed I used the wheelchair that's in the closet to wheel myself to the elevator. The elevators were right next to my room. Once I was in the lobby all I needed was a ride."

"And I was the first person you thought of," she interrupted.

"Actually I wanted to call Mitch . . . but yours was the only number I remembered. I'm thankful you came, though. I don't know who tried to kill me and I don't want you involved. So I need you to drop me off by Mitch's crib and he'll help me get out of dodge for a while. When I'm situated I want to come back and we can discuss a couple of things."

Kim wasn't sure if it was because she felt guilty about what happened to Jake or if it was because she never really fell out of love with him, but what she did know was that she wanted to be with him now. "It doesn't have to be like that, J.B. I could help you heal, we can leave here and start over somewhere else. You don't need this shit, baby, ain't nothing here for us. How could it ever be right for us here? You were given another chance; take advantage of it. We have enough money saved for me and you to keep driving and never come back!"

Jake was curious, "How much money are you talking about?" He really had no recollection of having any money put away.

Kim told him that it was at least $600,000. At that moment Jake felt proud of himself for having some stash tucked away, but he was surprised he didn't remember something like that.

"Where's the paper?" he asked.

When she told him she had it all in her possession he took a long pause, thought about it, and told her to just drive, but he knew in the back of his head, once he remembered everything that happened and he was in good enough shape, he would be back to finish what somebody started.

"I'm glad to have you back," she said. He was looking out the window when she said it but turned around after hearing the crack in her voice. When he looked at her there were tears running down her cheeks.

"What's wrong?"

"Before," she started, "you asked were we on good terms and I told you no. But the truth is we were doing really bad. When I had came to visit you in jail we had actually broken up." She paused before going on. "And when I was leaving the jail I had wished you dead. Later that day I got news of you getting stabbed and I felt like shit. I still feel that way. I felt like I put negative energy on you. I had to tell you this because I don't want you to hate me when you start remembering things. I swear I love you, J.B., but you had hurt me. I need you to understand that I was a woman scorned when I left you but now that you're back I will never let you go again. I prayed to God every day and night that He wake you up, and I swore to myself I would be the best woman to you a man could ever ask for."

Jake wanted to believe her. The things she said felt too real to be contrived. Besides, other than Kim, the only people he could remember having any real dealings with were his uncle Mitch and Mary-beth. *Oh shit,* he thought, *I wonder if M.B. came between us, or was it something else?* As he was thinking, gunshots rang out, shattering his thoughts and the rear window.

Kim screamed and was visibly shaken but didn't lose control of the car. About two car lengths back was a hooded up figure hanging out the passenger side of an old Acura letting a big-ass handgun go—it sounded like at least a .40 cal. Four more shots were sent flying through the air.

BOOM! BOOM! BOOM! BOOM!

Luckily, none of them found their target. Kim cried out, "God, please!" And prayers were indeed answered, but they weren't Kim's . . . they were Jake's.

Somehow this life-threatening situation jarred Jake's memory. Maybe it was because his life was flashing before his eyes, but he could see everything real clear now. As clear as if it was playing on a high-def television screen in slow motion. He remembered the robbery in the store. He remembered going to jail, getting the letter, having a fight, and getting stabbed. He even remembered every face. Then he snapped out of the past and back to the situation at hand. He asked Kim, "Are you hit?" "No," she said in a low whimpering voice. He looked out the rearview mirror. The gunfire had stopped for now but the car was still behind them. Then Jake saw something he thought he would never be happy to see: two squad cars with blaring sirens.

Mr. Hoody in the trailing car was unfazed. He came up with another burner—this one long and silver—and let it off at both of the cop cars. It sounded like New Year's Eve in China. Something about the situation made Kim flip. She knew she wanted her man and herself to live. She yelled for Jake to put his seat belt on.

Jake was spent; it took a lot out of him just to get out of the hospital, but he wanted to live. He clicked his seat belt just in the nick of time. Kim punched the gas pedal; the car sped up swerving side to side. The one behind them let off a set of shots that sounded like a young drumroll. The shots tore up a parked car. That's when Kim made the smartest maneuver she could have made by slamming down on the brakes. The trailing car rammed into her rear. It didn't flip like Kim had seen happen on TV, but it was enough to do the trick. The impact caused the shooter to drop his gun out of the window, then Jake heard more sirens. Just when he thought everything was going to be all right he heard: "Freeze. Get your hands up, NOW!" He looked out his passenger-door window and saw that the cops had the trailing car surrounded. He smiled, knowing that he had cheated death once more.

Jake took his eyes off the police, giving his attention to Kim. "Good driving, babe, you saved our lives." Then he knew what needed to be done. He had to find out who was trying to kill him. He had to get in contact with his uncle Mitch and Marybeth. He knew he needed to heal fast and he needed guns, too. He also remembered his nigga Nine-One.

"Put your hands up." This time the police were talking to them.

"We the victims mu'fuckaz; they were shooting at us," Kim shouted. "Get them guns out of our faces. And before you start with that bullshit about us coming to the station for a statement, I know my rights. We don't have to go anywhere."

The cops actually listened. Less paperwork for them anyway. "Sorry, ma'am, but we can't be too careful."

"Did y'all get them fools that were shooting at us?" Kim asked.

"Yes, ma'am, they're cuffed and in the car." When Jake heard that, he was relieved. Not that they were arrested—he wouldn't wish jail on his worst enemy—but that he would finally get some answers. This was the break he needed. Bits of his memory started to come back to him—near-death situations have a way of doing that—and he was going to get to the bottom of all this. He just hoped he would be able to heal up quick enough. The doctor said his hand would be fucked up permanently, but for some reason Jake felt a funny tingle in it. *Maybe* I'm *about to get some paper*, he thought. The thought made him chuckle a little bit.

"What's funny?" Kim asked. "How could you laugh at a time like this?"

Jake answered, "Sometimes you got to laugh to keep from crying."

The police told Kim and Jake that they would have to come to the precinct and give a report. Kim assured them that that wouldn't be a problem, then explained that she would have to do it alone and in the morning because her man had just got out of the hospital. The police said they understood—just some more black folks getting shot at.

PURE EVIL

Phil was standing in front of the bathroom mirror preparing
for trial. He was defending the CEO of a Fortune 500 company.
If he came out on the winning end it could be the biggest case
of his career, and he felt pretty good about a favorable out-
come. And why shouldn't he have high expectations? He was
fucking the judge who was presiding over the case and the DA
was a very close friend of his. After he pulled this one off, he
envisioned himself making about forty mil a year, not including all the perks: vacations, usage of the company jets, yachts,
five-star suites, call girls . . . the possibilities were endless.

   Phil worked hard kissing ass and cutting throats to get to
where he was. He had some of the most notorious crime bosses
in the world eating out of the palm of his hand, but there was

one little chink in his armor, one skeleton in his closet, and he needed to get rid of it. That skeleton was Jake Billings.

Phil had just gotten the news this morning and he couldn't believe what he had heard. There was no way Jake was still alive; he had heard of being lucky but this motherfucker had to have cat in his blood. Why was the man so hard to kill? "I should've finished him off while he was in that damn coma," Phil screamed at his reflection in the mirror. It didn't matter to him that deep down inside he knew he really owed Jake his life. And the funny thing was that Jake was the kind of guy Phil liked; the kind of guy he wouldn't mind going to a ball game with or just shooting some hoops with. Sure, Phil was a Jew, and Jake was a nigga, Phil thought at times, but they had so much in common. But as quick as those thoughts would arise, they would be overshadowed by this: The nigga has to die. *People supposed to walk around life knowing that they owe me a favor, not vice versa. Who the fuck is he?* And then there was that thing about Jake fucking his lady. Some how Phil couldn't get past that part. That and the daily nightmare he would have almost every morning—while he was awake.

The nightmares started the day after Jake saved Phil's life, back when Phil was defending Don "Phat" Murphy, who in Phil's mind had to be one of the sickest bastards God ever decided to put on earth. The best therapy money could buy couldn't make him feel sane after the whole ordeal. He could barely sleep and felt haunted every time he took a shower or endured any idle time. Not even Phil's eight-figure salary could ease his pain. He just wanted to forget the whole thing ever happened, and in order for that to happen, Jake had to die.

Phil convinced himself that that would be the only way to purge himself of the horrible memory. Jake was the link to a very deep, dark, and painful secret. If it got out, Phil felt it would ruin his career and his life.

A few years back, Phat Murphy and his ten-man organization were picked up on gun-running charges and distribution of heroin on school grounds. Everybody thought it was over for them, including Phat Murphy. Then a friend of his told him about a lawyer named Phil Rosenberg; one of the best Jewish attorneys in town. The friend said he cost a lot, but he gets charges dropped like weight from a fat man on crack. It didn't take much more convincing than that for Phat Murphy to hire Phil, and sure as shit Phil got Murphy and eight of his boys completely off; the other two took the weight for the rest of the crew. The two that laid down had no priors, which made it easy for the judge to justify giving them only three to six with the possibility of being home in a year and a half with good behavior. The not-guilty verdict sent a sense of power to Phat Murphy's head so great that only a bullet would stop it.

Phat began to think he could do anything and get away with it, and he did just that for about three years, with the help of Phil's counsel. But one day he went too far by deciding to use public school buses to transport his drugs from one side of town to another. He had both students and bus drivers on his payroll. This low-life stunt lasted about two years before the feds deemed his run was up. When Phil managed to have him raised on a million dollar bail, Phat once again thought he would beat the rap. Phil tried to explain to Murphy the next day during a private meeting that he held no power with the feds.

"I've been trying to tell you for years that all my power lies with the state," Phil said. "You're going to have to serve some time on this one."

"I spent over four million with you over the past five years, you better figure something out, bitch!" Phat Murphy was steaming hot by this point. "I gave your Jew ass five hundred gees of mine to put up in case something happened, right?"

"Yes, you have a retainer with me. And I've defended you and your friends relentlessly for years."

"Right," Phat Murphy yelled, ignoring Phil's argument. "Something just happened you dumb fuck—so get to defending. As a matter of fact," Phat Murphy spoke in a low, even tone, "I'm not an unreasonable man. I understand that I might have to pay a debt to society, and I'm willing to do that. But if I have to pay so do you. Being that I've given you around five mil up to this point, I figure you need to give me about half of that back. You can have the money sent to the same place you got the wire from. You can make the call now."

Phil knew that Murphy wouldn't hesitate to kill him. He was in Phat Murphy's office; they could have him murdered and buried with no one ever being hip to what went down. Knowing he was in a tight spot Phil tried to talk his way out of death's field of vision. "Before you try anything stupid with me, right, you should know that my secretary and about five other people know I came to see you. And forcing me to wire money is extortion—punishable by a lengthy prison sentence—trust me I'm your lawyer." Phil managed to muster a slight smile as he haggled for his life. "I said you would have to do some time, but that doesn't mean forever. I'm sure I can get you thirty-six months—forty-eight tops. I mean damn, Don, the charge you got carries forty years and I'm telling you that you may have to do three or four. No lawyer can promise you better than that. Do you know what it takes to get a federal judge in your pocket?"—No answer—"About ten to fifteen mil, and that type of money isn't easy to come by."

"Speak for your fucking self," Murphy said. "Stop fucking assuming shit you dumb Jew. I got the money to buy the judge so get to putting the bid in. And for the record," Phat Murphy added, "I hadn't planned on killing you or extorting you, I planned on blackmailing you, so make the call!"

Confused, Phil asked Murphy, "How do you plan on doing that?"

"I'm just kidding you now." Murphy laughed. "Earlier I was serious but you have put me at ease so I'm good now. I'll see you later. Here"—he pointed to a wooden box on his desk—"have a cigar and find your way out."

Phil took the cigar, thanked his client, and left the office feeling a little shook up but not scared. He knew big-time gangster types always went around trying to scare people shitless. A few of them were the real deal, but most of them were blowing smoke out their ass, and Don "Phat" Murphy didn't fit the description of someone who was intimidating or vicious. He wasn't believable in Phil's book. Phil had seen too many real gangsters in his time to believe this guy. To reassure himself, Phil thought of some of the reasons he felt made Murphy not so tough. One was the nickname "Phat" when the man was skinny as a rail. And the other? Well, why did all his friends call him Don like he was some kind of boss when his real name was Donald? "What an asshole that kid is," Phil said to himself as he rode down the highway. "I'm gonna make sure he gets every bit of time that he deserves. Then I'm going to blow that five hundred gees on a new Porsche and a couple of Franck Muller watches." Phil then wondered what Murphy's parents looked like; what their nationality was. Murphy was definitely mixed with something or other—a fucking mutt. How dare he fuck with me?

What Phil didn't know then was that Donald "Phat" Murphy was probably the most malicious man he would meet in this lifetime. His father was Italian and black, and his mother was Cuban and Polish. Somehow this fusion of nationalities afforded him the opportunity to connect with gangsters of all races. It was said that he personally liked to rape men that crossed him. And if that wasn't bad enough, he would videotape it and make his victims watch themselves being violated before he killed them. That was the exact plan he had for Phil. So when Phil's car pulled off the highway, so did the car that Murphy was in. Murphy wanted to keep up with Phil's whereabouts but he wasn't aware of the fact that he was being followed, too.

Phat Murphy either followed Phil or had someone keep tabs on him around the clock for the next two weeks. Doing so he learned that Phil had a thing for some black chick who owned a condo in the good part of town. Phil made it his business to get there at least four days out of the week. Murphy had the location of where he could snatch Phil from but maybe he would do this one a little different. *I'ma do this cracker dirty right inside his bitch's crib,* Murphy thought. *Then I'll do her right in front of him.* The thought made him feel that this may be one of the best tapes in his collection.

Murphy made the call to his crew and let them know tonight was the night it would go down. He had three dudes and a chick to play the condo and wait for the lawyer to return. "When he get there I want Betty to ring the bell holding a handful of flowers, like a delivery person. Once she gets that door opened you guys know what to do. I'll be on my way."

Phat Murphy's crew did as they were instructed and it went easier than they expected; they didn't even have to use the flowers stunt. When they went to the door the chick they had posing as the flower girl turned the doorknob to see if it was open first. It was, so she and her three accomplices ran up in the joint with their pistols out and totally caught Phil and Mary-beth off guard. They pistol-whipped Phil until he passed out, then stripped him and the girl of all their clothes and hogtied them.

Phil woke up shaken and confused. "What's this all about?" He attempted to get some answers for the madness that was taking place.

"Shut the fuck up," one of his captors said. "You'll find out soon enough." Phil did as he was told. Mary-beth laid there wondering what the fuck was happening. What had Phil gotten them into?

It took a little more than an hour for Murphy to show up; to Phil and Mary-beth it felt like an eternity. When he walked through the door he was all business. In a strange way Phil was happy to see his client. Maybe he could at least talk to the man; his goons were having none of it. "What the fuck, man?" He tried his hand. "What are you doing? What is this all about?"

"This is about me fucking you and your bitch up the ass,

recording it on my camera, and playing it back for you to watch. Afterward, I'm going to kill you both and watch the whole thing later on."

Hearing what these people had planned for them Marybeth started to scream, which only got her knocked out cold from a right hand to the left side of her jaw.

"Let's get this party started," Phat said, setting the camera up.

"Listen, man, this ain't necessary, you don't have to do this."

"I know it isn't," Murphy said, "but I want to do it. I want you to feel pain."

Feeling he had nothing to lose, Phil yelled, "You fucking faggot . . . I'm gonna kill you!"

Murphy laughed. "And how do you plan to do that?" he asked.

"Please don't do this," Phil begged. "Please don't do this . . ." His voice trailed off into a whimper.

All this was amusing to his antagonist. "Take him into the bedroom." A few members of his crew did as they were instructed. After Phil was removed from the living room the camera was set up in the other room. Murphy casually walked in behind his men. "I think you're gonna like this." He punctuated his statement with a series of punches, knees, and kicks until he was at the point of exhaustion. "Pick 'im up off the floor and put 'im in the bed," the boss ordered. Phil was hoisted off the floor, then the camera lens was adjusted, making sure the positioning was right. Then the unthinkable began. Murphy actually shoved himself up Phil's ass.

Phil let out an ungodly scream.

Murphy was about two minutes into the rape when he and Phil heard four gunshots. Startled, Murphy hopped off the bed, but he wasn't strapped. The door to the bedroom flew open and Jake walked in with a smoking gun in hand. Jake had been selling weed to Phil and Mary-beth ever since he'd met her at the mall.

Phat Murphy couldn't believe what was going on. "What the fuck are you doing here, J.B.?"

"I'm just visiting a couple of friends of mine."

"Mind your business and let me out of here and there won't be any problems," Phat Murphy said, causing Jake to bust out in hysterical laughter.

"You got some nerve telling me what to do right now you bitch-ass motherfucker. You're in no position to give out orders, especially to a man with a gun in his hand who just murdered four of your peoples downstairs. As a matter of fact, I got a few orders for you. First of all, untie that fucking man you nasty, perverted son of a bitch. You're a sick fuck and so is—well, I mean so *was*—them motherfuckers downstairs. Who the fuck do y'all think y'all are doing this kind of shit to people?"

Murphy thought about the past two weeks; the times when it felt like someone was following him, but he dismissed it as paranoia. "I'm that motherfucker that does whatever the fuck he wants to do," Phat Murphy boasted. "And you's a bitch-ass nigga. That's what this whole shit is about. You ain't just happen to stop by to check these people out. You did a good job with casing me and now you here to finish the job. You nothing but a small-time wanna be . . . a wanna be me. You figure you can stroll in here, kill me, and then take over my spots, but it won't work. You won't make it two weeks before you get gunned downed like you did my peeps."

Jake laughed in his face. "Why the fuck would I want to be

like your coward ass and go around raping people? Your whole style is chump. You got power because it was handed down to you. Nobody fears you; they fear the people you're connected to. You're a piece of shit that deserves to die. I actually wish I could kill you more than once." Then Jake aimed the gun at Phat's knee and pulled the trigger.

Jake pulled his knife from his back pocket and walked over to Phil, cut the wire he was bound by, and handed him his clothes. Phil was pretty shook up, but he was also filled with rage. In a chilling voice Phil said to Jake: "Let me borrow the gun." Then: "Where is Legs?" referring to Mary-beth.

"She's downstairs. I got here just in the nick of time; nothing happened to her. She is untouched if that's what you're worried about. His soldiers are instructed not to touch anyone until this sleazeball get his first—at least that's the word on the streets."

Phil aimed the gun at Murphy's nuts and squeezed off two shots. One bullet hit the target; the other shot went into the front of Murphy's thigh and came out the back. Phil set the gun down, walked into the hallway, and returned with a golf club. Phil swung the club so hard into Murphy's face that it make Jake grimace.

It looked like two gallons of blood flew out of Murphy's face, then Phil hit him about five to seven more times. The blows weren't fast or reckless, but slow and precise. Jake had no doubt in his mind that Murphy was dead. *Good for his ass,* Jake thought, then, "The tape has to be destroyed," he told Phil.

"Hell yeah it does," Phil agreed.

"You gonna have to move fast," Jake said. "One of your neighbors probably heard the shots and called the cops."

"No one heard anything. This whole place is soundproof. Once the door closes you can't hear shit outside. I had a mini gun range installed and I didn't want any complaints so I spent a pretty penny making sure no one could hear anything. So where do we go from here?" Phil asked.

"We destroy that video equipment first and foremost," Jake said. "Then we dispose of these five bodies and we forget this whole thing ever happened. You're a lawyer; you can figure out how much trouble we're in if we get caught."

"You're right, but I have one other request for you."

"What is it, Phil?"

"I don't want you to tell Legs what you saw up here. Tell the story like you got up here in time to spare me the embarrassment. I don't want anyone knowing what happened to me." Jake gave his word as a man that what he saw would never cross his lips and Phil promised to never say a word to anyone about the five murders. They shook on it.

"Now let's figure out how to get rid of these bodies without anyone peeping us," Jake said.

"I have an idea," Phil said. "I need a pickup truck and some of those long hockey bags that have wheels on them."

CHAPTER 11

HELP ON THE WAY

Jake wasn't sure if he was thinking straight after the latest attempt on his life. He had to find his uncle Mitch. He needed someone who could protect him and get him to a safe place. But most of all he needed to find out who wanted him dead or he wouldn't be around for long. It occurred to him that whoever it was must have had someone in the hospital watching him or there was someone watching Kim. That's when a wave of paranoia crawled up his spine. Why would Kim be riding around with that much money on her so nonchalant like she was used to having that much cash on her? She had no idea Jake was going to call. Was she is in trouble, talking all that "let's get up out of here and start over" shit? *Something isn't right,* he told himself, *I shouldn't trust her.* She did mention that they weren't on good terms. Maybe it was her who tried to get him killed in the first place.

Kim said, "We should be good here, baby." Jake acted as if her voice startled him. He was pretending to be asleep while he was contemplating whether Kim was trustworthy or not.

In a feigned groggy voice Jake asked her, "Where we at?"

"This is a Marriott hotel; it's about two hours away from where we started. I've been looking in the rearview mirror for the past hour; no one has been behind us for any length of time. And the police escorted us to the city line so I'm pretty sure we're safe here, for a few hours at least. We'll get moving again when it gets dark," she told him. Then, as if she had been reading his thoughts, she said, "You can trust me. I wouldn't do anything to hurt you—I love you! As soon as we settle in I'm going to call my cousin Tanya. She be in Mitch's gambling spot. She said she fuck around with his main man, Monster, but if I know that ho—and I do know that ho—she probably fucking your uncle Mitch and every other nigga in there with stacks." She said it like she didn't approve of her cousin's sluttish ways at all, but blood was blood. "She'll get your uncle on the phone for you, trust me, she has her ways." As she watched Jake she noticed that he didn't look too well. "You know you're going to have to see a doctor," she said. "You're not in a good condition; you could get very sick out here like this. We don't have to go to the hospital, but we at least have to see a doctor."

Jake looked Kim straight in her eyes so there was no misunderstanding. "No doctors . . . No hospitals . . . If I die, then it will be on my terms." This wasn't the time to trust anyone. "As a matter of fact, fuck this hotel—keep driving—we got too much money on us and I don't know who's who. Whoever is trying to kill me don't mind shooting at cops so I don't think two hours is quite far enough away. We better keep it moving," he said, and that's exactly what Kim did.

———

Meanwhile, back inside the jail, word was quickly spreading about Jake.

Everybody was talking; they knew he had awoken from the coma, escaped from the hospital, and came out on the better end of a shootout. Some of the guys started calling him Mr. Invincible. But the word wasn't isolated to just jail; it was on the streets, too, and there was no one more pleased than Mitch. His nephew was back and Mitch couldn't wait to see him. Where was Jake? He couldn't get that thought out of his head. Wherever he was, Mitch knew he needed help, so he decided to make a phone call from the hidden line he had in the Caddy. "Monster, hold the spot down until I get back. I have to make a trip to the other side of town. I won't be long."

Monster said that was cool and asked Mitch if he could pick up a bite to eat on his way back.

"Sure," Mitch said.

When Mitch got in his Caddy he made a phone call to the one person who might know what was going on: Mary-beth. He dialed her number and it rang twice before she picked up

She greeted Mitch with a, "Heeeeyyyy, stranger, long time no hear."

"Yeah, I know," Mitch said, "I don't mean to bother you, Legs, but I gotta get straight to the point. I'm hearing a lot of things on the streets and I would like to know if you heard or know what's going on with my nephew?"

"What do you mean, Mitch? I haven't spoken to your nephew for a couple of years; not since he was in jail. From what I heard he got out and moved away. I moved about two years ago myself—after I got pregnant—I had no real reason to stay around. To tell the truth this phone number is only the same because I was hoping your nephew would call it one day and I could give him the news about his child."

"Oh shit, Legs, the baby belongs to J.B.!"

"Yes, the baby belongs to J.B., and he never even called me. I thought after he got out of jail he would have at least said what's up, or goodbye forever or something you know. I know he had Kim and he knew that Phil and I had some shit going. I could never explain the relationship we had due to certain circumstances, but I only loved Jake. He is the only man I ever loved."

Mitch almost couldn't believe what he was hearing. He said to her, "You mean to tell me you don't know?"

"Know what?"

"J.B. was just released from the hospital after being in a coma for two years. Some gang motherfuckas stabbed and beat him into a coma while he was on the inside. From what I heard, he just got up and bounced. Kim scooped him from the hospital, but somebody else tried to kill him since then. The shooters were caught by the police and Jake and Kim drove off. I figured if he called anyone it would be you."

"I'm not into the life anymore. I gave up providing, um, 'helpful services.'" She chuckled lightly. "After I found out I was pregnant, I lost most of my connections . . . that life is over for me. I have a little one now." There was a pause, then, "But I'll help J.B. if he needs me. Will you do me a favor and let him know these things if you speak to him first?" The entire time she was talking it sounded like she was about to start bawling, and when she had nothing left to say, that's exactly what she did.

Mary-beth hung up the phone. She couldn't believe that Phil had lied to her about Jake being freed from jail. Two years in a coma. At that moment she knew in her heart that Phil was somehow responsible, and she swore she would make him pay for this bullshit, even if she had to get back into the life.

———

After five hours on the road, Jake told Kim to pull over at the next hotel. She pulled into the parking lot of a Super 8. "I'll wait in the car while you check us in," he said. "After we get settled, you can give your cousin a call to see if she can go to the spot and find Mitch." It was time to put a plan together. He knew there was no way he could keep running in this condition. He needed rest and he needed to recuperate—and he didn't really trust Kim one hundred percent. Something kept telling him that there was something she was hiding, but for now all he could do was pray that God stayed on his side and kept him alive.

When they finally got into the hotel room Jake hit the bed like a rock. He prayed for guidance and protection and hoped Kim didn't try to kill him in his sleep. He thought about smoking a blunt, then he was out cold.

———

"Damn that boy snore loud," the voice said. "Lucky you drove this far away. If y'all didn't they would've tracked y'all down from the snores." Jake was hearing his uncle's voice in his dream.

Then Jake heard Kim ask, "You sure you ain't hungry, Mitch?"

"Nah, lost my appetite thinking about all the killings and unnecessary shit we gotta do to survive in this world. Breaks my heart to have to see my nephew under these conditions. I'm glad he is still alive though, and I'm gonna make sure I keep it that way!"

"Music to my ears," Jake blurted out in his low, groggy Godfather voice.

"Hey, baby, we didn't mean to wake you," Kim said.

Mitch chimed in right behind her. "Sleeping beauty has finally awakened."

Jake asked Kim, "How long I been sleep?" Then he looked to Mitch. "How long you been here?"

"You've been sleep for about fifteen hours," Kim said.

"And I've been here about four or five."

"Damn," Jake said. "How the fuck could I sleep so long after being out for two years?" This sleeping shit was starting to bother him. "Kim, why you didn't tell me you spoke to Mitch and he was on his way?"

"When I finally got him on the phone I couldn't wake you up. I did what I felt was the smartest thing and that was get Mitch to where you was."

"Oh man, it's good to see you, J.B.," Mitch said looking his nephew over. "Damn you skinny as hell though, and your head is bigger than the rest of your body. But don't worry we gonna fix you up nice—better than ever before—and after that we gonna get to the bottom of this."

CHAPTER 12

MARY-BETH'S BACK

"The only hustlers in this world that live like they should are the ones fortunate enough to be around good businessmen like myself," Phil said over the phone. "So don't go jumping out the window like you're fucking crazy." He slammed the phone down before Mary-beth could get another word in.

The fucking nerve of her to call me and ask me anything. That bitch is lucky I don't know where she is or she might have gotten erased off this fucking earth, fucking cunt. I ain't heard from her stupid ass in two years and she calls me with this shit. Phil was still very bitter toward Mary-beth for calling it off with him like she did. She told him that she was leaving the life; she couldn't go on dealing with drug dealers, lawyers, judges, killers, whores, pimps, and every other motherfucker who needed her services. She was about to have a child. The thing that had Phil tight was that he knew the child wasn't his. Even though he and Mary-beth had never had a real relationship as far as marriage or an engagement, he considered her to be his—but he knew she didn't love him. She never tried to deceive him by saying that she did. In fact, if you let Phil tell it, he didn't love her, either. Their relationship was cool the way it was: They both knew the other fucked around with other people. But what was really eating Phil deep down inside was that he suspected Mary-beth had really fallen in love with Jake, a fucking weed guy, some corner thug. Out of all the guys in the world, why him? Why would she want a common hoodlum when she could have someone that was rich? And to make shit even more complicated, this was the same motherfucker who had saved him from that perverted killer, Phat Murphy; this fact ate at him from the inside out. *How could all this shit happen to me,* he wondered. His motto was: "Once Phil Rosenberg lays down with a bitch, she's his, until he tells her she's not."

———

Mary-beth was thinking up a master plan of her own; their daughter, Jocelyn, was almost two years old, and if Mary-beth had anything to do with it, her child's father was going to live.

Even though she'd put her old lifestyle behind her, Mary-beth still had love for Jake. Every time she looked at her daughter's eyes and smile, she thought of him. Many nights she missed her child's father, the coolest man in the world, the man who had once saved her in the nick of time—her hero.

What she did for a living before she left the life was a little of everything. If you were a lawyer or a judge and you needed female attention and wanted to get high, Legs was the lady to call. She could find you just the kind of woman you were looking for. If you were a drug dealer and needed a connect on weight, no matter what drug it was, she could find you a plug. If you were a thief and needed a place cased out or wanted the blueprints to somewhere, she could get that done for you. If you were a shooter, Legs would let you know who needed guns for hire. She was like a one-person agency for the underworld: good guys and bad guys alike.

When she found out she was pregnant, she just up and bounced from the life she was living. She wanted to start over with a clean slate. Money wasn't a problem. She had more than enough paper to be straight for life. But now things were different; this wasn't about money. This was about love.

Mary-beth called her sister Joyce and asked her to hold down her daughter until she got back from what she called her "business trip". "It's one that's going to keep me away for a few weeks," she told her. She knew Joyce would say yes because every day when they spoke on the phone, Joyce would ask, "When are you gonna bring that li'l angel over?"

Well, the li'l angel is coming because Mommy has to turn back into the she-devil, Legs thought as she got on her way. *Mommy is going to find her man.*

———

Mitch was sitting on the phone with the airlines setting up a flight for Nine-One and another flight for Dr. Nebbie, one of his old-school friends who was a natural healer and dealt with alternative medicine. Mitch knew that good ole Neb would want the money and he could get Jake back to good health and movement. He also knew that Jake wasn't with going back to the hospital so the deal would work out just fine for everybody. Mitch wanted Nine-One there because he needed to get back to town in order to try and get some answers to their many questions. And while he was gone Jake would need someone that he could rely on. Mitch had sensed that he wasn't exactly trusting Kim; with Nine-One there Jake might feel a little more secure.

Mitch told Jake the first thing he was going to do when he got back to the city was find out all the information he could about the dudes who were arrested for shooting at his nephew and the police. This would be easy for an old fox like Mitch, all he had to do was keep his ears open while motherfuckers spoke about everything they saw, heard, and thought about as they frequented his gambling spot. It would be especially easy to get the history on the jokers who shot at the police because that type of shit was held in high regard in the hood, sort of looked up to. What Mitch didn't know was that he wouldn't even need to keep his ears on alert because his man Monster already had the whole scoop.

Once Nine-One and Nebbie arrived at the hotel where Jake and Kim were hiding, Mitch prepared to leave. "Kim, it's probably going to be best if I take your car with me. Whoever is looking to kill Jake probably knows what he was riding in when he left the hospital." Kim didn't have a problem with the arrangements. Mitch left his car behind so Nine-One would have something to drive J.B. and Nebbie around in. Mitch hated to part with his Eldorado but it was mandatory for his nephew's sake. Mitch decided he would park Kim's car at the airport in long-term parking and get himself a first-class flight back home. Kim's Beamer was nice but it wasn't his style. Besides that, the back window was shattered and the rear bumper was scratched up, and Mitch wasn't into driving around looking hot or fucked up so he was on the next flight smoking.

CHAPTER 13

FLYING BULLETS

April 2010

Mitch's flight arrived right on time and Monster was waiting for him when he got off the aircraft. "You a'ight, OG?" Monster asked as they walked to where he parked the car he was driving. "Where's the Eldorado?"

"Yeah, shit is a'ight. I had to leave the Eldorado with my people: They needed it more than me."

Back in the car Monster lit up a freshly rolled blunt and passed Mitch an unopened pint of Henny. "Take a swig of this yak."

Mitch put the bottle to his mouth and took a good swallow. The potent cognac slid down his throat. "Whew, she biting." Monster passed him the blunt.

"OG, I got some info that you need to know."

Mitch took two long pulls of the blunt and stared at his protégé. "What is it?"

Monster picked up the cognac and took a swig. "I got the word on who tried to kill your peeps—J.B.—and they some serious characters, real foul dudes. They don't have regards for nothing—women, children—none of that don't mean shit to them. Motherfuckas so grimy they even do the family pets greasy. They call themselves the 300 Crew. How ever you want to go at them though, I'm riding with you one hundred percent."

"That's peace." Mitch thanked Monster for his alliance and then said, "I heard of the 300. I thought they were a bunch of young boys who started a little gang; when did they become so notorious?"

"When they started getting money out the ass and laying mu'fuckaz down like rugs and floor mats. Nobody even knows the real identities of these niggaz. Some say it's ten niggaz who can't be touched that run the gang. Some say it's three quiet dudes who each hustled up a few mil and came to the conclusion that if they got together they could run the city. Some mu'fuckaz say it's a cop that's running the shit. Some say it's a bitch . . . Truth is no one really knows who call the shots for them niggaz, or how many there are. Niggaz just know their name and their trademark, which is killing shit and supplying weight and committing all types of white-collar crimes."

"What the fuck has the streets come to . . . a bunch of mystery killers and dealers? You know what?" Mitch said in a serious tone. "I think about quitting the business; maybe it's time for me to move on. When all the smoke clears I might not even be around, know what I'm saying youngblood?"

"I feel ya, OG." Monster got in the right lane to exit the highway then asked, "Where are we headed: home or what?"

"Nah, I got work to do. I have to get to the bottom of who these 300 motherfuckers are."

"Where do we get started?" Monster asked.

"First," Mitch said, "we need to round up a little team of our own."

"So you want me to get hold of some live-ass niggaz that be bussin' them hammers?"

"Not at all, youngblood, not at all. What we gonna do is send a few chicks around to survey the land." Monster sat back and listened as his OG gave him game. "We gon' send our team of girls out to find out which bitches are buying the most Gucci, Louie, and Prada; who goes to the most expensive beauticians, drives foreign cars, and lives in nice cribs—and tries to stay off the radar at the same time. When we get that info we move on to the next step, young gee." Mitch had a smile on his face like he had it all figured out. "I betcha I figure out who these 300 motherfuckas are. I never heard of these motherfuckers running shit and no one knows them . . . some secret society gangsta shit. I ain't buying it—not on these streets—something gotta give."

Dr. Nebbie was a miracle worker, Nine-One was a lifesaver, and Kim was an angel. After three months, Jake felt like things were looking a little better for him, but it still was eating him up that somebody wanted him dead and he didn't know who or why.

The last thing Jake heard from Mitch was that the word on the streets was dudes who tried to kill him when he left the hospital were from a gang called the 300 Crew, which made no sense to Jake. As far as he could remember he got put in a coma because of the Northside Boys or, at worst, T.M.B. The reason that the whole situation spiraled out of control in the first place was because of the life-threatening letter he received. Why would so many people want him dead? He had been off the streets and running his little store for a minute. He didn't even own a car; he used Nine-One's car service. He lived a quiet life with his girl, Kim, in a modest condo. He could think of nothing in his day-to-day life that was a good reason for someone to want to kill him. Who in the hell had written that letter was all that was on his mind when ole Neb interrupted his thoughts.

"It's time to exercise," Nebbie said, handing him a cup of tea made from the nastiest herbs and spices Jake had ever tasted. This was the beginning of Jake's daily regimen, which consisted of drinking nasty drinks, having ole Neb stretch his body out for about an hour, then doing specific exercises that consisted of focusing on one muscle or joint at a time until Neb felt it was stimulated enough to move on. They were doing at least five different body parts a day.

Jake told Nebbie what the doctor at the hospital had said about his arm—how it would never work again. Nebbie laughed at the diagnosis and said, "We'll see." Then he started mumbling to himself real low in a language Jake had never heard before.

Jake was a lot more at ease with Kim than he was when they first left the hospital. For starters, she had explained the whole money thing to him. "Only about fifty thousand of the money is mine; the five hundred fifty thou belongs to you," she said. "I always kept it stashed for you, and I brought it right away because I didn't want you to think I was a thief. I would have dropped it off at your mom's house but there would have been too many complications." Jake kind of knew some of what she was talking about. His memory was far from great but some things were coming to him. He knew Kim no longer fucked with her mom real tough for personal reasons, but their moms always hung out with each other; it was nearly impossible to see one without the other. Kim continued to fill in some blank spots. "I been taking care of our parents' bills and pocket money for the past couple of years, but I kept receipts"—which were in the bag with the money—"for everything I spent. The only major purchase I made on myself was for the Beamer." She also said, "We have a joint account that I started with like forty grand in it, and if my memory serves me correctly you have about two hundred grand tied up in real estate some-where." She didn't know the details on that, though, because when Jake made those transactions they weren't on the best of terms. Jake respected Kim keeping it one hundred.

And Kim was proud of herself for keeping her own income a secret, even when she was having a soft moment for Jake.

Nine-One asked Jake if he wanted to go for a ride, but Jake declined. "Not right now," he said.

"Come on," Nine-One coerced. "You need the air and I need the company. I can't ride with Nebbie—I can never un-derstand what the fuck he's talking about." Jake and Kim cracked up when he said that. Nebbie even let out a chuckle followed by a stubby middle finger.

"Okay," Jake agreed, "I'll go, but I don't want to hear no sto-ries about your country and all that shit you always talking to me about, you fake-ass foreigner."

Nine-One smiled because he knew Jake was getting healthy and his mind was starting to remember the past. This was the first time since Nine-One had arrived that Jake had mentioned one of their debates. He thought Jake had forgotten about them, along with a couple of other things.

Nine-One was Indian and Egyptian, and you couldn't tell him that both of his races weren't the smartest people in the world. He was also a firm believer that those countries produced the finest women in the world. One day Jake grew tired of Nine-One complaining about the weather, the food, and the women . . . in this country, and said, "So why don't you go back to your own country?"

Nine-One gave him a wry smile. "This is my country," he said. "This is where I was born, but trust me I ain't too proud about it! One of these days I'm going to get a passport and travel abroad and see where I'm from."

"You mean to tell me you never even been out the country?"

"Not yet." Nine-One grinned.

"Then why the fuck you run around acting like you know about all these countries all the time?" Jake asked.

"Because I do," Nine-One stuck to his guns.

"How is that?" Jake asked.

Nine-One paused with a serious expression on his face, then broke into the biggest smile Jake had ever seen and said, "C-N-N, mu'fucka." He and Jake both busted out laughing.

"You ready to go?" Nine-One's voice right in front of him put a halt to Jake's reminiscing.

"Yeah, I'm ready. Yo, where can we find a bag of weed around here? I feel like I wanna smoke."

"I thought you would never ask," Nine-One said in a proper

tone. "It will be my pleasure to put something in the air." After they left the house and got in the Eldorado, Nine-One said, "There is something I want to tell you. I know you can't remember everything and all you're trying to do is get your memory back, but to tell the truth I don't think you should go back. I think you should keep moving. I've been driving you around for a few years and the money is great but I think it's time for you to move." As Nine-One was speaking, Jake started to get butterflies in his stomach and a lump in his throat. He had a feeling he was about to hear something he didn't want to hear. Nine-One continued, "Before your uncle Mitch called me to come up here, a friend of mine was telling me the story about you waking up from the coma and then the one about you escaping from the shooters after you left the hospital. The word on the street is that they've given you a new nickname: Mr. Invincible, which means when you get back home those who want you dead are going to work twice as hard. The word is that the 300 Crew wants your head and they got twenty-five thousand cash for anybody who can give solid info on you. And I'm going to be totally honest with you like I always have—I don't think your uncle is going to be able to help you."

"Why would you come to that conclusion, Nine?"

Jake was trying to get the back of the car seat upright because it was too far back, and he wanted to hear exactly what Nine-One was going to say, when two bullets came flying through the passenger window and missed him by a hair. Nine-One wasn't so so lucky. One slug caught Nine-One in the temple and the other slammed into his jaw. Maybe Nine-One had seen it coming because his foot had smashed down on the gas pedal and the Eldorado took off like a jet. Jake's heart was beating so fast he thought he might go into cardiac arrest. Nine-One was slumped over the wheel but he was a good driver even in death because his hands were locked tight on the wheel and the car pushed straight ahead. Luckily there wasn't much traffic on the road. Jake lifted his leg and put it over the dead driver's in an attempt to hit the brakes—it worked.

All the exercise had done Jake well. After the car came to a screeching halt, Jake threw it in park, grabbed the gun out of Nine-One's jacket, opened the passenger-side door, and hopped out, ready to shoot in what looked like one motion. His movements were so sudden that even he was shocked. There was no time to pat himself on the back, though; someone was trying to kill him—again. But there wasn't another soul or moving car in sight; just a bunch of parked cars. Jake held the gun straight out in front of him and spun around looking for someone or something to shoot. There was nothing, just Nine-One dead in the driver's seat and him standing there dumbfounded. Satisfied that the shooter was no longer around, Jake went to the other side of the car and struggled to move Nine-One from the driver's seat—then heard it.

BOOM—shotgun cocking—BOOM!

The shooter was a half block behind Jake and the car, walking toward him. *Where the fuck did this guy come from?* Jake wondered.

The shooter was walking toward him, letting the shottie go with the intensity of a man on a mission. Jake took cover by the front of the car. Nine-One's gun was a .357 Magnum, which meant it only held six shots and Jake didn't want to waste any of them. By the way the shotgun slinger was coming toward him, he was either born bulletproof, or had on a vest, or just assumed Jake wasn't strapped. Jake knew he had to do something quick. Not only was he in danger, but there was a chance that Kim and ole Neb might be, too—if they weren't already dead.

The shotgun slinger was tearing Mitch's car to pieces and Jake could feel him getting closer. Jake ducked underneath the car hoping to get a clear shot at his attacker's legs. He looked left, right, then straight, but the shooter was no longer there.

BADUMP! BADUMP! BADUMP!

Dude was hopping from car to car as if he anticipated what Jake would try to do. And as if things couldn't get any worse, now he was cutting loose with something automatic. Jake was feeling the wind and the heat ricochet from every bullet that was flying by him. Whomever Jake was dealing with was heavily strapped and obviously experienced in warfare. Unfortunately for Jake the Eldorado was in the middle of the street and his legs weren't strong enough for running yet. He had just started to walk fairly normal again, but after that the most he could do was a slow jog.

Pop! Pop! Pop! Pop! Pop! Pop! The shooter was still there.

Something hot hit Jake in the head, causing him to fall back. He actually thought it was over until he put his hand up to his head and felt it in one piece. A piece of metal from the car had struck him; not a bullet. Nine-One was just telling him about how the streets was calling him Mr. Invincible, and now his man was dead for nothing.

Jake sprung to his feet and dove toward the left side of the street. He gave it his all but it wasn't good enough to make him land behind the other car to keep him covered.

FUCK IT. *Might as well die letting off shots at this motherfucker. I ain't the type to die with a fully loaded gun,* he thought before standing up. His timing was perfect because the shooter was just tucking his automatic back in his jacket and was trying to grab the shotgun when Jake let loose the .357.

BLAM! BLAM! BLAM!

Two of the three shots rocketed through the dude's hip and the third shot missed, but the two that hit took care of business, knocking the dude from the car he was standing on. He fell and cracked his face on the concrete. He looked to be unconscious when Jake started to move in. After getting a couple steps closer, Jake didn't take any chances on this killer gaining consciousness; he let the remaining three bullets fly into the dude's head.

The whole ordeal left Jake exhausted, but he managed to quickly step over to the bloody body to check it out. The .357 slugs had tore the dude's face up so bad that even if Jake did know who he was, there was no way he would be able to recognize him now. He searched the body as fast as he could. Nothing. He took the shooter's automatic just in case someone else was waiting on him.

Jake knew that with all the gunfire that had gone down the police would be coming soon. He didn't have the strength to lift the shooter's and Nine-One's bodies from their spots in front of Mitch's car, and besides, Mitch's car was tore up from all the bullets that ripped through it. Jake had no intention of driving around in a car scattered with bullet holes; that's like asking the police to pull the vehicle over.

He made his way up the block in the direction the shooter came from. His reasoning was that maybe the shooter left a car running, and that proved to be one of the smartest thoughts he ever had because as the sound of the sirens were getting closer, Jake saw the shiny black Corvette. The car was running so quietly he almost missed it. Jake had his own theory on how the situation had panned out. He figured that after the shooter took his first shot and saw the Caddy come to a screeching halt, he probably pulled into a spot where he could watch his handiwork unnoticed. Once the shooter saw Jake get out of the car instead of Nine-One, he probably sprang into action, leaving the car running in case he had to get away in a hurry.

Jake would never know for sure, but it didn't matter. He hopped in, shoved it in gear, and peeled out in the opposite direction of the bodies. As he was driving he wondered, *how the fuck am I managing to stay alive?* There must be a good reason for it; did God have him here for some special reason? *Damn, I don't even have any kids to carry on my name.* He drove at high speed to get to Kim and ole Neb—he hoped they were all right. And it was at that moment he realized he didn't know how to get back to the hotel they were staying in. It was the first time he had been outside. He pulled over, took a deep breath, and asked God for guidance, direction, and forgiveness for playing a part in Nine-One's death. He even asked for forgiveness for the shooter he was forced to kill in order to save his own life, and while he was at it he even threw in Phat Murphy, his crew, and whomever else he harmed in his lifetime, then he peeled off and found his way back to the hotel.

When he walked in the room he found Kim and ole Neb sitting around watching television, oblivious to the fact that anything had gone wrong.

"We have to leave here immediately." Jake rushed the words out. He was exhausted from all the exertion.

Kim answered first. "What's wrong, baby, what's going on?" She rushed over to his side.

After giving them the abbreviated version of what happened while he was gone, Jake told Kim to give Neb fifty thousand dollars and suggested he go his own way; Jake didn't want to be responsible for anyone else's life.

When Kim tried to give Nebbie the money he put up his hands, shooing her off. "Mitch already gave me all the money that is required; there is no need for any more."

"It's cool," Jake assured him, "take the money. Let's just call it gratuities for the work you done on me."

"Okay, I'll take the extra money, but you take this." Nebbie handed Jake a book that contained the recipes for the nasty teas along with a few meals that Nebbie said would help bring him to a hundred percent. "Natural healing will bring your body, mind, and soul together." Kim handed Nebbie the money and gave him hug, a kiss, and a thank you. "You're welcome." He smiled and Kim ran back into the bedroom to finish getting everything together.

Now it was Jake's turn to thank the man who helped to restore his health, but before he could, Nebbie said, "You've thanked me enough. What I really want you to do for me is to try to get up and meditate in the morning and do the same before you go to sleep. It will help you get your memory back and give you a clear vision on how to go about certain things." Then ole Neb walked out the door. Jake wished he could meditate at that particular moment; he wanted to know why Nine-One said he didn't think his uncle could help. *What did he know, and why didn't he mention the twenty-five-thousand-dollar reward for the info on my whereabouts before?* Jake wondered. *Was Nine-One down with the other side?* No, he didn't believe that. *But was*

Nine-One trying to warn him about something or somebody? Mitch? Kim? Who is this 300 Crew, and why me?

"I'm ready," Kim said stepping out of the bedroom.

"I'm going to need you to get Nine-One's things together." His stuff was in the room adjacent to theirs. When Kim went into the other room, all she saw was a zipped-up backpack. The closet and dresser drawers were empty. He'd never unpacked. She grabbed the backpack and left the room. Jake met her outside.

"You ready to get out of here?" he asked.

"Sure, this place was starting to get me a li'l stir-crazy anyway. Where are we heading though?" she asked as they hopped in the Corvette as if it was their car. Jake had to drive because Kim didn't drive stick.

"We ain't going nowhere," Jake informed her. "I'm dropping you off at the airport and you're gonna get a flight to a different coast." Before she could interrupt he said, "Right now I don't know how they keep finding us but they do, and I can't risk losing you." From the look on Kim's face Jake was positive that it wasn't Kim who was trying to get him killed. He could feel the love she had for him; it was in her eyes. He felt like shit for mistrusting her.

Kim was crying. She had waited two years to be with him again and now he was trying to send her away. "Why can't we just leave together on the plane and try to hide?"

"We tried hiding, and Nine-One is dead for my efforts. Something has to be done. I'm going home so whoever wants to find me ain't gotta look far."

CHAPTER 14

BIT OF TRUTH

Jake turned to Kim and asked her: "You don't have any ideas or hear anything on the streets about who wants to kill me?"

Kim answered: "Pull the car over" in a tone of voice Jake had never heard from her. He pulled the Corvette over on a somewhat empty road with feelings of paranoia entering his body. He knew something was wrong. Kim looked into his eyes; she looked as if she thought these would be the last words she would ever say to him. "Baby, I want you to understand that the way I feel about you is real. I truly love you more than anything, and living life the way I've been living it for so many years has become difficult."

Jake interrupted her. "What up, Kim? What you trying to tell me, baby?"

Kim didn't say a word. Tears dropped from her eyes. Out of nowhere she jumped out of the car, and yelled, "You can't trust Mitch!" Then, as she fell to the ground, in a God-forgive-me-for-what-I've-done voice, she said, "You can't trust me, either!" As she said that, Jake knew he was in even more trouble than he had thought.

"WHY THE FUCK SHOULDN'T I TRUST YOU OR MITCH, KIM?"

"Because we've both betrayed you before, Jake!"

"How?" Jake demanded.

"We had an affair," Kim blurted out.

Jake was shocked and at a loss for words. He grimaced—his face looking as if he had just inhaled and tasted the nastiest shit in his life. Kim could almost see the steam coming off his head. Jake told her, "I don't believe this! When did this happen? When I was in a coma? Before that? ANSWER the fucking question, Kim!"

"We'd been messing around for a few years off-and-on before the coma," Kim replied sadly.

"How the fuck could you do that, Kim?" Jake asked. "Was you trying to get me back for M.B.? You fucked my uncle to get revenge on me?"

"Jake, I don't know why I did it to be honest with you. Maybe she's the reason, I don't know," Kim said with a shrug of her shoulders. "But don't sit there and act like you ain't do me dirty time after time! Our whole relationship was a joke to you!" Kim started getting loud like she could feel the pain of the past running through her body like a cold gallon of water.

By Kim's reactions and her body language, Jake thought maybe she was telling the truth. *But my uncle wouldn't do that.*

Mitch was too real to let a woman come between them, but anything was possible and he wasn't putting anything past anyone right now.

"Kim, get in the car! We're getting out of here. It ain't safe for us to be staying still like this."

Kim did as she was told and they drove off. For a couple of hours no one said a word. Jake started to ponder, to put things together in his mind. As they got closer to home, Jake felt relieved that he hadn't put Kim on the plane. He never would have the answers or the info he needed. Before they got to their destination Jake asked Kim, "Why you trying to play me for a fool? What's the real deal? What's really going on? There's been three attempts on my life and you're gonna try to throw me off? I just got out of a fucking coma and you gonna pull some shit like you and my uncle fucking? Besides that, are you lying about the money, too? I didn't have no five hundred fifty thousand dollars! Whose money do you have and why you keep lying?"

It was dark out and the parkway they were driving on was mostly empty. With the frustrations of being a marked man and really wanting the answers to his questions rolling through his mind, Jake pulled over and faced Kim. "Make your decision," he said. "Is this the spot you wanna die at?"

Kim started to protest, but before she could get the words out Jake caught her with an open-palm blow to the forehead, then grabbed her throat with one hand and wrapped his other around her pinky finger. "I'm gonna ask you again. Is this the spot you wanna die at?"

Kim could tell by the look in his eyes and the energy he was giving off that he would do it. He would kill her right here. She regretted telling him about her and Mitch, but she couldn't hold it in anymore. She said, "No Jake," shaking her head like a toddler desperate not to get a beating. The inside of the Corvette on a dark parkway was not where she wanted to die.

"Listen to me good then, Kim! Are you telling the truth about Mitch?"

"Yes," she whimpered in a little-girl voice. "I said that so you know to stay away from him. You think he's a good man, but you can't trust him."

"Who's trying to kill me?" Jake asked. He started to bend Kim's finger back with the intention of breaking it. He wasn't feeling her answer. How could she sleep with his uncle and how could he sleep with her? Jake was enraged. He never felt so hurt and betrayed at any other time in his life. He wondered if it could get any worse. Then it dawned on him that maybe that's what Nine-One was trying to school him to. *Maybe that's why he said he didn't think my uncle could help me. He knew what was going on with Mitch and Kim?*

Kim was crying hard; her eyeliner was running and her shirt was soaking wet from a mixture of tears and sweat. She was scared for her life.

"Shut the fuck up, you dirty bitch," Jake yelled.

During all of these years Jake had never laid a hand on her. She didn't expect him to get violent. "It was Phil Rosenberg. He had me set you up, Jake! He's the one trying to kill you! I'm sorry, baby, I'm so, so sorry!"

"You fucking bitch," Jake whispered. *Snap.* Her finger was broken. "How you like those apples, bitch?"

"Jake, please please please please stop!"

"Please what, Kim? Why did you do it?" *Snap.* "Now that's your ring finger you fucking bitch! I can do this all night, Kim!"

Kim yelled, "Stop please! I did it because of your baby, Jake. I wanted you to hurt like I was. I'm supposed to have your child not that BITCH!"

"Mary-beth has a kid by me?" Jake asked his question with a look of confusion on his grill.

"Yeah, Jake. A li'l girl."

"And that's why you want me dead? Because of that, Kim? Is that worth getting a nigga killed? Huh? So how much did you sell me out for?"

"That five hundred fifty thousand that's in the trunk. Please stop hurting me," Kim begged. "I will tell you everything, Jake."

Jake could tell Kim was being truthful from the sound of her voice. She became too weary, couldn't take the pain any more. He was actually thinking to himself that he should kill her and leave her right there, but he decided not to. He let his grip of her throat and fingers go before he went too far and killed her for real.

That was exactly what Kim was waiting for. Without hesitation she reached to her side and came up with a .38 revolver with no hammer and aimed for Jake's head. She felt she had to kill him because he was on the verge of killing her. It was a move purely based on self-preservation.

"Motherfucka, stop hitting me," she screamed.

"What the fuck?" Jake yelled. He smacked the gun from her hand. In the process, a shot went off and hit Jake in the leg. He didn't feel it but he knew he was hit. The gun ended up on the floor on his side of the car. The Corvette was a tight fit for him so as he was fidgeting around to get the gun, Kim, scared for her life, jumped out of the car. "KIIIMM," Jake yelled. "Get the fuck back here!" Jake hopped out of the car and tried to see where she was running to and what was around.

BOOM BOOM BOOM BOOM.

Four gunshots suddenly went off. "Jake, help! Help!" Kim was screaming.

"Where are you?" he yelled, pulling the automatic he took from his last victim off his waist. "Where are you?" Jake couldn't believe what was happening.

BOOM BOOM.

Two more shots rang out. Jake's right leg felt hot from the bullet he'd caught in the car and he felt he was on the verge of falling out. He looked down at his pants and noticed two holes, one where the bullet entered and another where the bullet exited. "Oh shit," he said to himself, but he had to block out the pain. "KIIIMM!" No response from her. He was hoping she wasn't dead. Then he saw her about fifty feet away, laying in the street, and ran over to her. "KIM! KIM, you a'ight?" She was laying facedown. He turned her over. "Kim!" From the looks of it she was done. Jake counted three bullet holes in her. He put his hand under her nose to see if she was still breathing. She was.

In a voice that was a little lower than a whisper Kim said, "I'm so sorry, Jake! I didn't mean for this to happen."

"Ssshhhh! Sshhhh! Just hold on, Kim. You gonna make it. Stop talking!"

Kim knew she wouldn't make it and felt horrible for setting Jake up. She would try to make it right before she passed on; this would be her last chance to confess her wrongdoings.

"Jake, listen to me! Don't go back! Keep moving. Besides Phil wanting you dead, there's other people who want you dead. Phat Murphy has family who runs that 300 Crew. I don't think you can trust anyone. You're a marked man!"

"Take it easy, Kim! Tell me later. We got to get you to a hospital."

"Please listen to me, Jake!" Kim was stressed. "I loved you and you've always been good."

Three more gunshots went off in rapid succession. This time Jake saw where it was coming from. A Corvette that looked just like the one he had been in was flying toward him with the shooter hanging out the passenger-side window squeezing off something large. Jake let every shot off he had in the automatic and it didn't stop a thing. They were still speeding toward him and Kim. The only thing left for him to do was to try to pick up Kim and move out of the way. As he attempted to pick her up, he prayed that God would spare Kim's and his life and allow them to make it out of the situation they were currently in. He felt God was listening because he scooped up Kim and moved out of the way in the nick of time, as the car barreled past them. Jake hoped his bullets touched the shooter in the passenger seat and that the driver decided to just keep it moving.

He wondered if those were Phil Rosenberg's people. Maybe it was Phat Murphy's brother or maybe it was the people who sent him the mystery letter in jail. Jake looked down; Kim wasn't looking good. He thought she was dead until she coughed up blood.

"Hold on, baby! Hold on, you're gonna make it! You're gonna make it," Jake repeated over and over in her ear until they reached the car. As he put Kim in the car all kind of thoughts were running through his head. Then he raced to the hospital. He didn't want to go there but he knew time was against them and his choices were limited.

As Jake was driving, he noticed three more Corvettes in the rearview coming toward him. "You gotta be fucking kidding me," Jake said. Then he looked over at Kim, and he knew she was dead. "Fuck!" He tried shaking her hoping he could get her up, but it was over. She was gone. He had a lump in his throat and a sharp pain in his chest. He was furious and had a taste for blood. He was feeling under his seat for the .38 that had landed there, while keeping an eye on the Corvettes. The cars were gaining on him, which was exactly what he wanted. He finally found the gun. It had five shots left. Jake let the cars gain on him a little more. Then he pulled into the right lane and made a quick U-turn. He was now headed northbound in the southbound lanes with the pedal to metal. He was going straight toward the three cars that were after him.

"Y'all motherfuckers ain't got to chase me. Here I come!"

Jake was on the verge of insanity. He was over the edge. Nothing mattered anymore. Kim was dead. It was partially his fault and to make things right he was gonna kill as many people as possible. He drove toward the car in the left lane. "Let's see if you wanna play chicken, motherfucka!" The drivers of the triplet 'vettes didn't expect, nor were they prepared for, the move Jake made. It was instant death for whomever he crashed into. The impact would tear both cars to pieces. The 'vette in the left lane, which was normally the right lane, had no choice but to go left, which caused him to smash into his partner's rear end in the middle lane. That caused two out of the three 'vettes to spin out of control. The one that was in the far left lane couldn't do anything but speed up in order to not get caught up with his two partners. Jake did the smartest thing he could think of and continued northbound on the southbound side. "Thank you, God," he whispered because no cars were coming toward him. He reversed up the nearest exit. His heart was pounding and his head was ringing. His leg was bleeding and Kim was dead. Jake had to ditch the Corvette. He knew nowadays there were cameras in almost every streetlight, and police were probably gonna be looking for any black Corvettes on the road. He still wasn't sure how the fuck these people kept finding him. *Why would Kim trust Phil Rosenberg for anything?* This had to be the work of this so-called brother of Phat Murphy who wanted him dead. Phil was a lawyer, which meant he was too smart to have a team of killers. One or two yeah, but a team? No fucking way!

Jake was determined to make it. He had a child he had to see. "Where the hell is M.B.?" He felt awkward thinking about that with Kim dead in the passenger seat, but it was what it was. Jake had only two options. The first was go to his mom's spot; the second was going to his and Kim's old crib. He chose to do the second. Maybe there were some clues or something he could use to find out how to get to Phil and Phat Murphy's brother.

———

Meanwhile, in Phil Rosenberg's office . . .

"Are you still holding that grudge against me, Frank?"

"Why would I hold a grudge against you, Phil? You gave me my life back. If it wasn't for you I would still be in jail, and when you got me out, you put me on payroll. So no, I don't hold any grudges. If anything, I appreciate all you have done for me, Phil!"

"Well I hope so, Frank, my man, because I have a feeling the shit's going to hit the fan pretty soon. I never heard back from his li'l girlfriend, which was expected after that little shootout. That 300 Crew sure is relentless. Why couldn't they wait until he was settled down? Why try to kill him at the hospital? That made no sense!"

"Hey, Phil, tell me something. How did you get his girl to turn on him?" Frankie was really interested in the answer; curious what made a woman flip on her significant other. He never got to ask his wife or his brother how it happened or what he did to deserve that.

"Well, Frank, first I let her know about the child he had with Legs. Second, I let her know Jake was about to be picked up by the feds and she was going to go along for the ride. Third, I let her know that if she worked with me, nothing would happen to her. Then I threw the cherry on top with a nice payment. It all made sense. All she had to do was get him somewhere, settle down, chill out for a while, and I would handle the rest. With Jake out of the way she wouldn't have to worry about doing time. You can get a scorned woman to do a lot of things, especially one who is scared to go to jail."

"Wow," Frank said before adding, "Don't worry about a thing, Phil. I doubt he comes back. Only an insane man would come back to look for death. You probably won't ever hear from him again."

Phil replied, "Trust me, we're going to hear from him again! He survived too many attempts on his life. He is gonna want some get-back, and to tell the truth I can't blame him. It's partially your fault for not killing him in jail when you had the chance, Frank! He might remember who you are and come back to find you."

Frank replied with, "If he does, he does. But I guarantee you he won't make it! I will definitely kill him this go-round! Phil, how would he know you set him up? If the girl is setting him up, why would she say something?"

"Well, Frank, my friend, I believe she told him. Maybe she wouldn't have said a thing if the assholes didn't fuck up! But I'm pretty sure she told him something by now. There have been two attempts on his life since his escape from the hospital and he's not a stupid man. He'll soon figure out that she's the one who gave up his whereabouts, and that is when the shit is going to hit the fan."

Phil had no idea how right he was until his personal phone rang while he was talking to Frank. Frank could tell something was wrong. Whoever was on the other end of the phone was delivering info Phil didn't want to hear. Phil hung up the phone and took a seat before speaking again. Then he said, "Speaking of the devil! Can you believe this motherfucker is back in town? Can you fucking believe this guy escaped death again? How can so many people fail trying to kill one dude? Not an army. Not a posse, but *one* man!"

"Maybe he's just lucky," Frank replied, kind of taking Phil's remark personal. "Because where I hit him he should have died, but he didn't. Some things are hard to kill and sometimes it's just not your time. There are men who have been in war for years and come home untouched. Then you have those who die the first time they step on the battlefield. A strong will and a strong spirit is hard to break! But you don't have a thing to worry about! I'm here to hold you down and I guarantee Jake's will and spirit ain't stronger than mine. In all due respect the guy doesn't seem like a bad dude. Kind of a stand-up guy it seems. Why do you and this 300 Crew want him dead so bad?"

"Why is that your concern?" Phil shot back. "I have my reasons and there is more than one! I'm gonna be good to you, Frank, and I'll give you some incentive to make sure you keep me alive and get this guy dead." Phil walked over to a painting on the wall and removed it. There was a safe in the wall. He punched a code on the number pad, opened it, and came back to his desk with five hundred thousand neatly piled in fifty ten-thousand-dollar stacks. "After he is dead, you get the other half."

Frank had never seen that much money in his life. "Thanks, Phil! I really appreciate this and I'm gonna take care of you." Frank was a happy man. There were times he thought of killing Phil for the grimy bastard he was, but something told him not to. Besides getting him out of jail, Phil had given him a well-paying job—and a million was a come-up and half a mil in hand felt incredible. He was glad his brother had fucked his wife and he'd tried to kill both of them, because if that hadn't happened he would never have had the money he was currently touching.

"I'm gonna take this money, Phil, but I need you to be on the up-and-up with me if this thing is gonna work! I'm gonna need you to listen to the advice I'm gonna give. I know you like to live a lavish lifestyle and go out and party a lot, but them kind of things are gonna have to be put on ice for a minute. It's bad enough you work in the courthouse, which is downtown in the center of everything. So, we have to be on extra point going to and leaving that building."

"Okay," Phil said. "I got you. Don't worry about me playing it too easy and acting like a fool. I take my life serious. That's why I'm paying you so much. I have witnessed how diligent Jake Billings is, so trust me, I'm going to mind my p's and q's, my friend! I suggest you don't underestimate him. I know you're a master of martial arts, and have a military background, but this kid is more dangerous than your average street punk!"

"It's no problem," Frank said. "He lived through it once, but he won't make it again when I get my hands on him!"

CHAPTER 15

POP OFF

Back on the other side of town...

"Fuck it," Jake said. He was going home. He was gonna throw all caution to the wind and go to the crib. If someone was waiting for him there that would be a risk he was willing to take. He had five shots left in the .38 and if Kim hadn't got rid of shit he had a few more hammers in the crib, and he knew he had to dress up his wounded leg. Thank God the bullet went in and out because he refused to go to the hospital. He had to ditch the car. It wouldn't be smart to go to the crib with his dead girlfriend in the passenger seat. Jake needed help, but had no one to turn to. He wasn't feeling well. He had a lot of people to deal with and it was a shame that his uncle Mitch was one of them. He had never crossed Mitch and he couldn't imagine why Mitch would do that to him. But he would soon find out.

He told himself thinking of Mitch wasn't going to help right now. *I need a bright idea,* he thought—and he came up with one. He was going to park at Phil Rosenberg's office, at the back of the building where the visitors parked, and leave Kim and the Corvette there. By doing that he was leaving Phil a little message that he was back in town. He figured he could call a cab prior to getting over there, then simply park and grab the three book bags he had with him, which were Nine-One's bag, Kim's bag with the money in it, and his bag.

The intensity of the situation Jake was in made him think clearer than ever. Somehow he could remember the phone number to the car service Nine-One worked for, as well as the numbers of everyone else he used to call, including Mitch's and M.B.'s. He had to chuckle. "A li'l funny how I remember shit during the oddest time! God, thank you, for I know it's You helping in my time of need!"

He made the call and requested an SUV or family-size van—those cars looked less suspicious, especially in the middle of the night. He wasn't trying to be spotted. Time was of the essence, so after he called the car service, Jake rushed over to Phil's office. He wanted to be parked before the cab got there so the cab driver wouldn't see where he came from. It was almost 4:30 in the morning. He was pretty sure there weren't too many people on the street and doubted Phil was in his office. Jake parked in visitor parking. He threw his hoody over his head, so low it damn near touched his top lip, to avoid a good picture in case there were any cameras rolling. He took black sweatpants out of his bag and threw them on to cover up his bloody pants, then grabbed the three book bags and the .38. He was out the car and standing by the parking lot entrance for no longer than a minute and a half when a green minivan pulled up. It was a mid-90s Nissan Quest, which was right up Jake's alley. He threw the luggage in the backseat and followed behind it. After telling the driver where to go, he was on his way. Jake felt horrible about leaving Kim's body behind, but he had no real choice in the matter, and in a few hours the authorities would find her anyway.

The van turned two corners and as it passed the front of the office, Jake saw two figures. He couldn't quite see their faces, but by the body language and the way one was walking down the steps, he knew one of the dudes was Phil Rosenberg. Jake's hand was on his burner and he was ready to hop out, but he knew that wasn't the smart thing to do because of the time, place, driver, and his injury, and because he didn't know who the other person with Phil was. The other figure did seem familiar, though. Jake couldn't pinpoint it, but he had the feeling people get when they're around an enemy, that jungle instinct or sixth sense. He told the driver to make a U-turn. He had to get a good look at the other guy.

The driver did as Jake asked. As they passed the front again, Phil and the dude were close enough for Jake to look at their faces, and he did. He saw Frank's grill, and chills ran up and down his spine as if he could feel the pain from that brutal altercation they had in jail.

Jake was staring at one of the two men who put him in a coma and was now walking with Phil Rosenberg at the crack of dawn. "What the fuck," Jake said to himself. He felt like risking it. Five shots, he figured; that's two for each of them—but what if the guy with Phil was strapped? Jake couldn't count that out. He took a deep breath and told himself, "Patience is a virtue and you will get them another day! So be cool for now." Then he took another breath and thought about Kim being dead in the car and all the attempts made on his life. This was too good of an opportunity to pass up. So Jake said fuck it and told the driver, "Pull up to those two dudes." The driver obeyed, even though he had no idea what was about to happen. As he pulled up, Jake threw the sliding door open. "Hey, remember me?" and Jake let off two shots at Frank. PAPP PAPP. One to the head, which only grazed his ear, and then another to the chest plate. If Frank would have had a bull's-eye on his chest, it would have been directly in the middle. A perfect shot.

Phil was already running and screaming, "No! No! Help!" Jake let off the other two shots at him. PAPP PAPP. They hit him directly in the back and floored him. Then Jake put the gun on the van driver. "Drive."

"Okay, okay, okay! I got you! I got you, c'mon, fam, please don't hurt me! Please don't hurt me, fam," was all the driver kept saying.

"I ain't gonna hurt you! Chill the fuck out," Jake told him. "Gimme your cellphone." The driver did as Jake demanded. Jake thought he was bugging out when he looked out the back window. The car had some distance, but he saw Frank get up off the floor and walk toward Phil who was also getting up. "Damn bulletproof vests," Jake said to himself. "I thought the first shot was a head shot, though. Damn, my aim must be off! They got the message, though!"

Jake reached into the bag and pulled out ten stacks, then threw them in the driver's lap. "Pull over in a few blocks and get out. Give me twenty minutes before you call the cops. Sorry to put you through the trouble, my man, but those were bad guys that deserved it! I had to do what I had to do."

"I feel you, fam," the driver said. "I wouldn't have called the police and told them shit! I would have just reported a stolen car. I know who you are, fam, even with that hood over your head. As soon as you spoke and I heard your voice I knew who you was."

"How you know that?" Jake asked.

"I used to shop from you. You gave me and my seeds mad discounts, plus that motherfucking Nine-One use to always brag about you. How he didn't need mad customers, how you paid better and was mad cool, how he was the first to have the Caddy truck 'cause you was holding him down. How he was picking up rappers from the airport and bringing them to your store. That motherfucker praised you like Jesus!"

"Good looking," Jake said. "That ten stack should buy me like a hour right, fam?"

"No doubt," the driver answered. "No doubt!"

Jake told him, "You tell the police exactly what happened. Just make sure you don't give them my description." The driver had no intention of telling the police it was Jake who did it. He had street principles. Never tell or you can never come outside! That's how he grew up. Sparky was twenty-four years old and from the projects. He drove cabs because he already had a felony and wasn't trying to go back, but there was no way in the world he wasn't going to tell his homies what happened. He just witnessed Jake Billings, aka Mr. Invincible, do some incredible shit. Damn that nigga was crazy!

Sparky had heard a lot of shit about Jake, but from seeing

him in the store you got a different impression. Just a cool dude. So he thought some of those hood stories were exaggerated, but he seen it live and in person tonight. As he was thinking, amazed by the events that just happened, a Tahoe came to a screeching stop and the windows went down.

"Where the fuck is he? Which way did he go?"

All Sparky seen was a man with blood on the side of his face looking angry with a brand-new 9mm, so he smartly replied, "I don't know! That asshole just jacked my fucking car! Please don't shoot me! I'm a cab driver. Am I gonna try to kill somebody and get out and walk? Hell no." Then: "Please don't hurt me!"

Frank rolled the window up and pulled off. He couldn't believe he almost lost his life. Thank God he bought those vests, but he almost got his head blown off. He picked up the phone and called Phil. He told him to stay put. He said he'd be right back after he spun around the block a few times to make sure the coast was clear.

Jake pulled the minivan into a pharmacy parking lot. He went in and got gauze, medical tape, alcohol, peroxide, a first-aid kit, then hopped into a local cab with his three book bags. He knew he couldn't go to his crib now. That was out of the question after what just happened. He told the cab driver to take him to a liquor store—where he purchased a sixty dollar bottle of Courvoisier—then he told the cab driver take him to the airport. He was going to take a room in one of those cheap motels out that way. The kind where a hundred dollars was your ID. Another hundred could buy you peace, quiet, and anonymity. Jake needed time to rest and let his leg get better. It was only a flesh wound. All he had to do was clean it up, wrap it up, and chill for a week or two.

Between what happened with Phil and his friend and Kim and the guys in the Corvettes, Jake was exhausted, and hungry, too.

Jake found a little mom-and-pop operated motel with a white attendant. There were four white families living there, three black old-timers playing cards in the lobby, and two middle-aged women speaking Spanish who looked like they were supposed to be the staff. It was perfect. He paid for a room for a week and went down the hall. First thing he did was call for something to eat. The little attendant answered the phone.

"Yellor!" That was his way of saying hello. His voice was crazy, Jake thought.

Jake asked him, "Do you guys have a kitchen here?"

"Yup we do," the guy answered. "What ken I do fo ya?"

"Can I get a steak, eggs, and some potatoes, and a pitcher of water and four orange juices?"

"Yup. Yes, sir. Ya shur can! Be there in forty-five minutes, sir."

"Thanks," Jake said. Then he grabbed all three book bags and the bag of shit he got from the pharmacy and went and sat on the tub. He peeled his sweats off, then the bloody pants, and carefully placed them in a garbage bag. He wasn't sure why, it just seemed smart to be cautious.

Jake wasn't digging the way he was smelling at all. Besides having dried blood on him, he had sweat a lot and had a really funky odor. He poured himself a big cup of Courvoisier and downed it. That was the only painkiller he had. Then he poured alcohol and peroxide all over his leg and bit down on the towel to refrain from screaming. He looked at the clock and made a mental note of the time. The man had said his food would be there in forty-five minutes. He'd used up about eight of them already. He didn't want to look like he was doing something suspicious when whoever brought the food came to the door. So he hopped in the shower for fifteen minutes. He did his best to clean his wound, got out of the shower, bit the towel, and poured more alcohol and peroxide on his wound. He spread some Neosporin ointment around the little holes and taped the gauze around his leg. He turned the television on and threw on the sweat suit he had in the bag. He did all of this and still had ten minutes left. Not really, though, because soon as he sat down there was a knock at the door. Jake peeked out of the viewer, then opened it wishing he had bullets for that .38 because it would sure make him feel more secure.

"Here we go, butty. A nishe hot meal for ya."

It was the attendant from the front desk. "Thanks," Jake said. "How much I owe you?"

"Twenty-five dollars for the meal usually, but first one on the house for customers here over a week."

"Thanks," Jake said. "I appreciate that."

After the man left, Jake sat down, ate, and took another drink. He would contemplate his next move after some rest. But before he went to sleep, he needed to go through Nine-One's and Kim's bags to see if there was anything in there to assist him on what he needed to do. He grabbed Kim's bag first and emptied the contents onto the bed. She had a box full of bullets for the .38—*glad I found those,* he thought—the money, a couple of sweat suits, bras, panties, and toiletries. Then he grabbed Nine-One's bag and emptied it. Nothing of significance, just clothes. So Jake decided to load up the gun, then go to sleep for a few hours.

Jake tried to sleep but he couldn't. He had too much on his mind. He knew he had to handle his business, wounded or not. Plus, he couldn't stop thinking about the fact that he had a child by M.B. Since he couldn't sleep, he decided he would call her from the cab driver's cellphone. He let it ring four times. She didn't pick up. He called right back and let it ring another six times. This time she answered with a curious hello. Jake said, "What up M.B? How are you doing?" Without giving her time to answer, he followed up with, "Is it true we have a child together?"

She coolly answered, "I'm fine, and yes we do." Even after all this time, even though she had so much to protect, Marybeth couldn't front on Jake. She had to come correct. "Jake, I wanna apologize for not being any help to you. I thought you were free and skipped town! When Mitch let me know about you being in a coma and people trying to kill you, and how he was looking for you because you was in trouble, I felt like I was in the twilight zone!"

Jake had been through so much he couldn't trust her or anyone for that matter, but he had no choice but to try to find out the truth. For all he knew she could be working for Phil, too, and the whole baby thing could be a setup. He had to think out what he was gonna do.

"Listen, M.B. I need you to meet me in the airport by the food court tomorrow around ten A.M."

"Jake, that could be dangerous," she replied. "I know what's going on and who's trying to get you. That might not be the smartest move to make. You should get out of town. Whatever moves you wanna make, come back and handle them. But right now you should stay low! You have reasons to live. You don't have enough manpower to go to war!"

"You don't know what kinda manpower I have," Jake replied. "I'm enough manpower! Me alone! I don't need no army and I wanna let you know if you're included in this grand scheme for my demise, I suggest you get out of it! If you trying to lie to me about this child of ours I will treat you like an enemy and all my enemies better stay low!"

"You fucking listen," M.B. said. "I understand you've been through a lot of shit, but I ain't the one trying to cross you! I'm the one that loves you! The one that has always loved you for Christ sake! You're my child's father and besides that, you saved my life before and I'm grateful for that. So get it through your thick skull, I'm not trying to harm you." She hung up the phone.

"Damn crazy-ass chick!" Jake was talking to the tone. The phone rang back. It was a message, a picture mail message. When Jake opened it he saw the most beautiful little girl in the world. He knew she was his. She had all of his facial features with M.B.'s complexion and hair. Then the phone rang again and it was M.B.

"Do you still think I'm lying? Do you still think I got some-thing to do with you being hurt? I need to know Jake! I can un-derstand if you do, being in the situation you're in, and if that's the case I can go back home and raise our daughter all alone! But if you do want my help, together we can figure out how to handle all of your business in the correct form and fashion! What you did this morning was dumb! They're talking about you in damn near every hood. Your cab driver was from the projects and you know how that goes! But you're hot! You should stay low. I'm close by but not in town. Text me a list of things you need and I will get them. I got to go now. I got work to do!"

"Yo, M.B.," Jake said, getting her attention before she hung up.

"Yes, Jake."

"Thanks a lot! I'm sorry for giving you a hard time, but shit is real right now!"

"I know! We'll get through it, though, and Jake I want you to know that I am truly sorry for your loss! You have my condolences for Kim."

"How did you know?" Jake asked.

"It's on the news. Been on for the past two or three hours. They found her body in a Corvette in Phil's visitor's lot."

Jake switched the channel from the show he was watching to the news, and there it was. "Oh shit! Call me in the morning, M.B." He hung up the phone. Then, realizing how short life is, he called M.B. back and said, "Where's my daughter? I wanna see her. I wanna see her now!"

M.B. said, "We can get outta here, drive away, and leave this godforsaken place behind and raise our daughter as a family. Fuck everybody! I have enough money put away for us to have a great life! Shit, I have a great life right now not far away from here!"

Jake was tired of the game. He now knew he had a seed to live for. He thought about it and told M.B., "You know what? The shit sounds good. It sounds like the smart thing to do. I wouldn't mind starting over! I'm tired of being around here anyway! Tell me where you at and I'm gonna catch a cab there and we're gone!"

"Are you for real, Jake? You ready to leave now?"

M.B. was happy and Jake could hear it in her voice. "Yeah I'm for real. We are out of here! I already got two years to try to make up with my baby girl. I might as well get a jump on things!"

M.B. told him where she was at and Jake took a cab over there with his book bag full of money and the .38. When Jake got to M.B.'s spot, he knocked on the door. She opened it with a big smile and a hug and a kiss. "Oh my God, Jake, it's been so so long! You still look good, baby!" She wouldn't let go. "Damn, I'm sorry all of this shit happened to you," she said in a sincere voice. "You didn't deserve any of this!"

She explained to him how she up and cut all of her ties because of their child. He explained everything that he could recall that happened to him from the robbery of the store up to calling her on the phone. M.B. cried like a baby. She felt for Jake. "Jake, I know you're hurting, but the best thing to do is leave. It's the only thing that makes sense."

———

Back in Phil's office, Phil was screaming into his phone at his secretary. "Leave me the fuck alone! I'm not taking any calls today!" He slammed the phone down. "Frank, what the fuck are we gonna do? Can you believe what this son of a bitch did? He almost killed us! If you didn't make me put on that vest I would have been a dead man, and for that son of a bitch to leave his dead girlfriend in our parking lot shows how fucking crazy he is! Now the feds are gonna be sniffing around here for a little while trying to figure out what the fuck is going on! I want this guy dead real soon."

"Yeah, I want him dead, too," Frank replied. "And I agree: the sooner the better!"

Frank wanted him dead so he could collect that other five hundred thousand dollars, and by the way this guy was acting, it wasn't gonna be a simple task. He was reminded of that fact by the nonstop ringing in his ears and the occasional tingling where the bullet had grazed his head.

Phil interrupted Frank's thoughts. "I want you to come to a meeting with me later, Frank. Not as security, but as a partner of mine. I want you to meet a few people. Since you're a part of this, you need to meet the guys!"

"Who?" Frank asked.

"The 300 Crew. Even though they are the most powerful organization in the city, for some reason Mr. Billings keeps getting around them. Now we have to have a meeting to figure out how to bring this problem to an end. We need closure."

Frank had heard Phil talk on the phone with members of the group, but he didn't know Phil had meetings with them. He'd heard of the 300 Crew and had actually seen their crew take over every other crew in the jail, but he never saw a leader or knew or heard of anyone besides Phil who knew them. He even remembered the kid, Dollar, who was the leader of the Northside Boys, talking about getting down with 300 and getting big time. Those guys were like phantoms on the street. You heard and seen what they did but no one knew who the bosses were.

CAN'T RUN, CAN'T HIDE

M.B. updated Jake about the 300 Crew. How their power reigned across boundaries that the typical criminal only dreamed about. Whatever territory they wanted, they took over. Whoever they wanted dead . . . died. They had the law on their side, judges in their pocket, and they even scared the shit out of the toughest criminals the streets had made. Their main methods of getting to most people was by threat or physical harm to a loved one. They did not believe in the street princi-ple of: No women or kids get touched. It was basically every-body and anybody could get it. That's how they got so powerful and came out of nowhere and took everything over.

"How many members in this Crew?" Jake asked.

"I don't know. I haven't gotten that far yet in my research. I believe there's only a few of them. Their anonymity is what makes them so powerful. If people knew who they were it would make it easy to get to them," M.B. stated. "So once we find out who one of them is, I'm pretty sure we can figure out the identities of the rest of them."

"I really need to know," Jake told her. "I'm leaving now, but I will never live life comfortable until this is over. So I will be back to handle this."

"At least we know Phil's out to get you so he must be somehow connected to them," M.B. replied. "You said Kim said don't trust your uncle so maybe he's connected also. But what's puzzling me is this brother of Phat Murphy's, who is he?"

"That's what the fuck I been wondering about," Jake said. "Shit, I been wondering was Kim telling the truth at all! The shit makes no sense. How would Phat Murphy's brother know I was involved in his brother's death and not know Phil was? I only got into that shit in the first place because of Phil, and we got rid of all of those bodies together. So either Phil lied to Phat Murphy's brother or Kim is lying." And what Jake still couldn't figure out was what part his uncle Mitch played in all of this. *And who the fuck sent that letter in jail? Was it the dude he shot in front of Phil's office, the guy who put him in the coma?* All of this shit was really getting to him. Why did people want him dead so bad? It had to be something he was missing. Something else he did that he couldn't remember.

"Fuck it," he finally said.

Jake asked M.B. if she had any weed. He needed to get high to relax his nerves.

"You know I keep some weed. I can't wait to smoke it," M.B. answered. She pulled a rolled up dutch out of the console of the rented Impala she was driving and sparked it up. Then, to brighten the convo up, she told Jake, "I can't wait until you see your daughter, Jocelyn! She looks juuussst like you!"

———

At the same time Jake and M.B. were discussing their child and their future, Phil and Frank were headed to their meeting. Frank was eager to see the dudes who ran everything. Phil told Frank: "Don't speak until spoken to and try to remember their faces. I have a feeling we are gonna have to take one of them out one day!"

"Why would you say that?" Frank asked.

"Because I get a feeling when I'm around those guys!"

Frank asked, "Where we going?" as he noticed where Phil was parking.

"Right in there," Phil said, pointing to a church. "You surprised those who do the devil's work meet in the church? Well don't be! This type of shit has been happening since the beginning of time."

Frank felt reluctant to go in. He wasn't willing to sell his soul to get money. There was a lot he was willing to do, but he wasn't sure about this. Phil, sensing what was going on with him, said, "Listen, Frank, all we doing is talking and that's it. It ain't like you selling out God or something. Come on, Frank."

Against his better judgment, Frank said, "Okay, let's go."

Phil and Frank walked into the church. When they got to the room the meeting was in, Frank noticed there was a big square table with three king-size chairs at the head and about ten regular chairs around the sides. He figured whoever sat in the big chairs were the leaders. Frank felt kind of funny about being one of the first people in the room, especially since he didn't know anyone. Phil looked at Frank and said, "Stop worrying!" Then another man entered the room. Frank recognized him immediately and was shocked. It was CO Frazier. Frazier gave him a nod and took a seat as four more men came in behind him—Mitch from the gambling spot and three guys he'd never seen before. All the men greeted one another like they knew one another for years before taking seats at the table. One remained standing—his name was Albert Murphy.

"Who the fuck is this guy?" Albert asked, glaring at Phil.

"Hold it. Hold it," Phil said. "We have company today!"

Frazier interrupted. "Easy, Albert. This is the guy who put Jake in that coma two years ago."

"Thank you, Frazier," Phil continued. "This is Frank Butler, and he's my bodyguard—a black belt in three different martial arts. From now on, he's working with me personally."

"Yeah, but what the fuck does he need to be in our meeting for?" Albert asked, knowing good and well that Phil trusted him as much as he trusted Phil—not at all.

Frazier wasn't feeling this pissing contest. "Butler! Welcome! That was some good work you put in on that guy. I'm surprised he lived!" Frazier turned toward the rest of the guys. "We could all use someone like him in our crew, agreed?"

"Agreed. And that brings us to our business here tonight," Phil said. Frank was surprised how Phil took charge of the room, and while Phil was speaking Frank figured it out. Phil was the boss; he was the leader of the 300 Crew. When he spoke they listened—even Albert Murphy, who spoke next.

"You're right. Let's get to the point. This Jake Billings is becoming too big of a problem. We need him dead and we need it fast. How can one guy be so hard to kill? On top of that several of our members are dead! Kim is gone and there's no telling what she told this guy!"

Mitch interrupted him, "The bitch is dead because she didn't follow orders! If she would have done what she was told we wouldn't be meeting right now and she would still be alive."

The first guy got irritated by what Mitch said. "You was around him, too, Mitch! You had plenty of opportunities to put him down yourself. You might be getting soft! So I wouldn't be so cocky about talking about a bitch I killed, especially if I was fucking her! And what kinda dude are you to be fucking your nephew's girl anyway?"

Phil spoke again. "We going to the next plan. We have to get to his mom or M.B. and her baby. Other than that we don't stand a chance of getting to this guy. Any objections anyone?" There were none. "Well, everybody use your resources and let's make something happen!"

———

Jake couldn't believe how beautiful his baby girl was. "Damn, M.B., I can't believe how much she looks like me!"

"Yeah I know. Looks like you spit her out. She has your demeanor, too," M.B. said.

"I wish I was there when she was born. I can't believe I missed so much of her life! I'm glad I'm here with her now, you know! Looks like you did a great job with her."

M.B. smiled. "Why thank you, Jake! I appreciate you saying that! I have so many pictures and video footage to show you of her. I'm so glad you're here with her, and me, too. I know it's a lot of things we have to handle, but first I want you and her to get to know each other."

"Sounds good to me," Jake replied as he spun Jocelyn around and she laughed.

"You know from the second I laid my eyes on this li'l angel I understood why God allowed me to make it and not die."

"I feel you," M.B. agreed. "It's a beautiful sight to see you and your daughter together. I didn't want to raise my child without her knowing her father. God made you pick up the phone and call me. That's why we're here together now!"

"I believe you're right," Jake said, still playing with his daughter. "But what if I didn't call you? What were you gonna do? How long were you gonna wait around for?"

"Are you forgetting what I used to do?" M.B. asked. "I damn near had the key to the city. I would have found you one way or the other. And I didn't expect you to call. I was there to get some insight of my own. I wanted to hook up with some old connects and see what I could find out. After I spoke to Phil and asked why he lied, and he wasn't acting like a gentleman, I figured I needed to get to the bottom of a few things."

As she was talking, M.B.'s house phone rang. "Hold on, Jake, let me get that. It's probably my sister calling to let me know she got home safe."

M.B. ran to the phone in the kitchen. "You thirsty or hungry? I can get you something while I'm in here."

"Some juice, please," Jake answered. Jake was looking around at M.B.'s house. It was crazy. He suspected she was living good but she was really sitting pretty. Her house could have been on "MTV Cribs." She was only an hour and a half from the hood, but Jake had never heard of this place. It was like they were somewhere people go to hide.

"You want lemonade, OJ, or cranberry juice?" M.B. asked from the kitchen.

"Whatever; it don't matter," he answered. Jake made a mental note that there was a phone in the room he was in and M.B. could have picked up that one to take the call, but she didn't. Then he told himself that he shouldn't be so paranoid. When she came back in the room she had a weird look on her face. Jake noticed. He passed it off as him being paranoid.

"Here you go! I mixed the OJ with the cranberry."

"Thanks," Jake said. "M.B., this house is extremely nice. You have great taste."

As he was talking, someone knocked on the front door. By the look on M.B.'s face, Jake knew something was wrong. He handed Jocelyn to M.B. and grabbed the .38.

"No, no! It's not like that," M.B. said. "You can put that away. Please put it away!"

"What's going on?" Jake asked.

"I think it's my boyfriend."

"Why didn't you tell me about him?" Jake asked. "You forgot or didn't consider this would happen. I'm not feeling this!" Something just didn't feel right.

"Listen, Jake, I told him I was leaving town and I would call him when I got back. I don't know what made him come by."

Jake looked M.B. in the eyes and said, "Listen to me! I'm tired of running. I'm tired of hiding. I'm tired of people trying to kill me and I'm tired of being double-crossed. Now I'm not sure if you're trying to pull a fast one. I'm gonna give you the benefit of the doubt because I don't think you're stupid enough to try something with this beautiful baby girl around."

"I'm gonna go upstairs and put Jocelyn in her crib. Then I'm going to the front door and tell him to leave and I don't appreciate him coming over without calling first. I'm a grown woman with a child and he needs to respect my space," M.B. said.

"A'ight," Jake said. "You do just that and I'll be standing right behind the door. If that don't work out and something funny happens, he gets it. Then you get it and I leave with my baby."

"Jake, I'm not lying to you!"

Jake replied, "I hope for your sake you're not."

KNOCK KNOCK KNOCK KNOCK KNOCK. M.B. and Jake looked at the door. "Go put Jocelyn upstairs and come back down and get rid of him." Jake was starting to get a really bad feeling. He didn't want anything bad to happen, especially to his daughter.

M.B. came back down the steps halfway with a terrified look on her face. With her cellphone to her ear and a nine millimeter in each hand, she waved for Jake to come to her. She was frantic and said in a whisper, "There's four of them out there. One at the door and three around the house. It's not my boyfriend. I don't know what the fuck is going on but I don't like it! I called nine-one-one already."

The guy who was knocking at the front got tired of that and attempted to kick the door open. Jake had had enough. He wasn't waiting around to be killed. He told M.B.: "Go upstairs to Jocelyn." He took one of her two guns and walked to the door with plans to let off two shots. The guy behind the door beat him to the punch and let off four through the door. All of them nearly missing Jake's head, causing him to hit the floor. M.B. didn't waste time and returned fire through the door. Then she ran upstairs.

Jake was in a trance. He felt stupid for even going with M.B. Why would he go in the vicinity of his child knowing that death was chasing him around? Nine-One was dead and so was Kim. The thoughts of his dead peeps made Jake say, "Fuck it!" He got off the floor, and since whoever it was didn't shoot back after M.B. shot through the door, he opened it and stepped out with two guns up. One pointed to the right, the other the left. He saw no one. He ran around the sides of the house and the back and didn't see a soul. Jake ran back to the front. He made sure to not catch one coming through the door so he yelled out: "M.B., it's me coming in," and went inside. "They're gone!" he told her.

Jake knew at that moment he would never be able to have peace of mind. His only options were to kill or die. The events that had recently taken place in his life were getting to him.

"M.B., I'm sorry I called you and got you in this mess! I know you was trying to hold me down and help me out but you know as well as I do this shit that's happening is crazy! Phil has to die and whoever Phat Murphy's fam is has to die also, or I have to die. But somebody's gotta go!"

M.B. responded as honestly as she could. "If you go back again you might not be as lucky as you were last time. But if you don't kill them they're gonna kill you." M.B.'s phone started ringing. "It's probably the police!" She picked up and terror enveloped her face as if the devil was on the other end.

Who is it? Jake wondered. The voice on the other end asked her: "Were you scared? Did you fear for your life? If you and that bastard baby wanna live get the fuck away from Jake!"

M.B. screamed: "Who the fuck are you and why the fuck would you do that, you sick motherfucker?" The man told M.B.: "Shut the fuck up and just tell Jake to come home or next time things won't be so nice. Matter of fact, pass the phone to him you fucking cunt!"

M.B. said, "Here," to Jake and handed him the receiver.

"Who this?" Jake asked after taking the phone and putting it to his ear.

The voice said, "It's me. I wrote you twice when you were in jail. I never got to carve you up, though, due to the fact you got put in that coma. But now that you're up and at 'em again, I figured I would pay you a visit. I'm surprised you're still alive. You have to stop running to your girls for help. That's not a good look for you!"

"Who the fuck are you and what the fuck do you want with me, you fucking pussy! First you write me letters in jail like a bitch and now you're calling on the phone like it's a joke! Why didn't you come through the door, you fucking dick? I would have murdered you!"

The man on the other end of the phone, in a sincere voice, asked, "Are you fucking kidding me? You're a fucking joke! Only reason I didn't come through that door is because I didn't want to kill that pretty young lady and her daughter. Plus I was just letting you know I'm back! You already have enough enemies! But I'm the one that's going to finish you off."

Then the mystery man hung up. Jake looked at M.B. and said, "This shit is unbelievable!"

"Who is that and why does he want you dead?" M.B. was frightened.

"I don't know the answer to either question. All I know is that he wrote me letters in jail on how he was going to get me, but other than that I don't have a clue! I was thinking it had to be Phat Murphy's brother 'cause Kim put me up on the fact that he wants me dead, also, but that don't make sense 'cause the only people who know about that is me, you, and Phil!"

At the moment he said it, the lightbulb went off in his head. He pointed his gun at M.B. and said, "Put your hands where I can see them," with the voice of a drill sergeant in the military. M.B, understanding just how real it was, did exactly as she was told. "You don't even have a boyfriend, do you?" Jake asked as he took the gun from her.

"No, I don't," she answered.

"Who was that you was on the phone with in the kitchen? Please don't make me get nasty with you, M.B.! Please! I need the answers and if anyone has them, it's you. There's some things I want to know and you're gonna tell me."

"Listen," she told him. "I have been honest with you until the moment I got in this house and that phone rang. When I picked up they told me they were here and said if I didn't set you up to stand in front of the door they was gonna do things to me and my baby that I couldn't imagine. He asked me who's life was more important to me, the baby's or yours, and I only had a few moments to think about it. When I saw the guys on the monitors I wanted to tell you, but I couldn't. I was too scared."

Jake could hear the sincerity in M.B.'s voice and stopped pointing the gun at her. He sat in the chair. He was defeated. There was no one left in the world he could trust.

"I'm so sorry, Jake!"

"Yeah," he answered. "I hear you but I gotta go."

Jake wanted to kiss his baby and get a good look at her in case he never saw her again. He had a good idea of what was going on. Not all the way, but he was smart enough to figure out that Phil had somehow got to Phat Murphy's brother. He made it look like it was Jake who was responsible for his brother disappearing off the face of the earth and excluded himself. *There was no way this guy would be that determined to kill me and not Phil,* Jake thought. He still needed to figure out how Kim got involved and why his uncle would cross him like that.

After seeing his daughter for what might have been the last time, Jake told M.B. goodbye, grabbed his book bag and the keys to her rental car, and drove away.

CHAPTER 17

GAMBLING MAN

Mitch's gambling spot,
one day later

"All bets are down," Mitch yelled out. He had the dice in his hand and Monster was housing. There was at least one hundred to two hundred thousand dollars circulating in the spot and he wanted all of it. "It ain't my thing to gamble." Mitch was talking shit as he was rolling the dice. "I only do this once in awhile but with that kinda money involved shhiittt! I wasn't gonna pass up trimming y'all young boys' pockets. Plus I got so much money, so many employees, so many bitches if y'all didn't know I was one of the biggest bosses in the world, I figured I'd show you tonight! It amused me that y'all would even bring y'all money here to lose like that against a c-lowologist like myself tonight! How stupid can y'all motherfuckers be to go against leadership like this?"

He was laughing as he was talking and joking around with the younger gangsters. He was playing with them. Nothing they ain't heard before. To them it was just dice talk, but in his mind and to himself he knew the shit he was talking was true. Reminiscing, he could remember the day the 300 Crew idea came about. It was like it had all just happened yesterday.

Kim and Mitch had been fucking around behind Jake's back. Mitch felt bad that it was Jake's girl he was fucking—he truly loved his nephew—but there was something about Kim he couldn't resist, especially not when Jake seemed like he was trying to dead it all—get out of the hood and get away from Kim. Mitch could tell that Kim was the type of chick always hungry for more—more money and more power. She had girls boosting for her and had a couple others stripping. She owned a few properties and was still running the smoke hustle Jake put her on to years back. In Mitch's eyes, she had taken full control of things while Jake kept a low profile in the store and chilling at their condo—avoiding the real motherfuckers.

The night Kim came to check on him, Mitch could tell she was serious about something. She walked in his gambling spot, lit a blunt, took a long pull, and walked up to Mitch and shotgunned the smoke down his throat. She sat him down on his sofa, threw her jacket on the floor (and her Prada bag on top of it), and lifted her long sundress off of her body, standing there completely naked. Kim straddled Mitch and shotgunned the rest of the blunt smoke down his throat. Mitch was usually on top of his game, but this had completely stunned him; he could barely move but to inhale and to lean into her, when Kim's last shotgun turned into a long, passionate kiss. *Damn, she tastes good,* Mitch thought, as Kim pulled away, getting off his lap and walking over to her purse, reaching in for the two flasks inside.

Kim moved back to her spot on Mitch's lap and took a big gulp out of one of the flasks. She grabbed Mitch by his cheeks gently, tilting his head back to give him her mouthful of liquor, following it up with another deep, slow kiss. She repeated each sip in this way until both flasks were empty. During this whole ordeal neither she nor Mitch said a word—not until after she'd pulled Mitch out of his pants and began to ride him.

"A man like you shouldn't have to touch much. People should be doing things for you. I'm tired of just fucking you. I want more for both of us."

"More? More like what? And what about your man?"

"Yeah, there's Jake, but I ain't thinking on that note right now. We can get around that. He too cool and content with whatever the fuck he doing—which is nothing much nowadays. I got plans, Mitch, and it involves a lot of bread."

Money always made Mitch's eyes light up a little brighter—and the yak in the flask or the sensation of Kim throbbing against his dick didn't hurt, either.

Kim continued, "But I need a man like you behind me!" and she started to quicken her pace.

Mitch grabbed her waist, holding her still for a second—just a second so he could grasp what she was trying to say. "What you talking about, Kim?"

"Just listen, Mitch. I'm talking about taking over, taking over without getting dirty and without getting caught up. I'm talking about me and you and few other people getting together to make a *real* power move! Now shut up and let me finish."

With that, Kim went back to riding Mitch hard and smooth until he exploded.

As they laid on the sofa, smoking that bomb after-sex blunt, Kim went on, "Mitch, I need you to shut down the spot one of these days so I can hold a private card game. And I need you to be my partner."

―――――

The night for the private card game came and Mitch could remember how Kim shined among some of the area's most powerful men—men like Phil Rosenberg, that crazy rich attorney who was known to be strong in the courts, and the Calvin brothers, who had a rep for being strong in whichever endeavors they chose to be in. Everyone knew you didn't cross them boys if you didn't want to be physically harmed—on top of that they were said to be related to Albert Murphy, the most connected man in the city. Albert Murphy's name rang from the mayor's office to every street corner. He was it—the don! Mitch couldn't believe Kim had them all present. She even had CO Frazier there, the most respected CO from the jail.

Kim wasted no time laying out her purpose. She asked the room, "Do you guys know what it takes to win?"

Albert Murphy, most amused by the little black girl with the very big mouth, said, "Enlighten us, honey. What does it take?"

"One hundred percent offense. One hundred percent defense. And a game plan that's one-hundred proof. Three hundred percent, gentlemen."

Everyone nodded. The lady was on to something.

Kim continued, "The way I see it, everyone in this room is

powerful, but Mr. Murphy, Mitch, and the Calvin brothers and myself? We have a lot to lose if we get caught up. Now Mr. Rosenburg and Mr. Frazier, you guys aren't in risk of losing much—if anything—given your connections with the long arm of the law. But there is much to gain if we work together, pooling our resources, and distributing our risks. I have a pretty good hunch you guys are willing to be involved—in your line of work, you have to be a little crooked to be any kind of successful."

As all the men chuckled at her joke, Kim continued to layout the plans for their new organization. Like an exec for a Fortune 500 company, she had it down to a tee: how everything would work if they put all of their powers together; how they could run their shit like a crew of phantom bosses, the kind you only hear about in myths, the ones you're not sure really exist. Catching on, Mitch added, "Police can't arrest the boss if the workers don't know who's employing them."

Kim shot Mitch a smile, and winked at him. "Exactly. No one would expect all of us to be working as one. Not even the feds will know who to look for."

The plan was so solid that no one in the room could resist. Phil thought it was amazing money. Mitch could see nothing but more money, and Kim's ass on top of him as soon as the meeting was over. The Calvin brothers were with it, and Frazier was hungry to rake in the dough and have the reign over the jail that he *knew* he should have. Even Albert Murphy was convinced that Kim's idea—the 300 Crew—was brilliant, even coming from a woman. "Hey, Mitch," Albert said, "Go get a bottle of something nice—Louis XIII nice. It's time to make a toast, to the 300 Crew!"

———

Mitch's thoughts were interrupted by Monster. "C'mon Mitch! This a forty-five-thousand-dollar roll. They got the bank stopped. Bust them motherfuckers in the head."

Mitch blew on the dice and said, "Get 'em bitches," and rolled 6-6-6. "Yeah, I told you motherfuckers! Watch out now them bitches is baaad!"

"That's what I'm talking about!" Monster cheered his boss on. "That's what I'm talking about! Ninety thousand in the bank. What they down?"

"I got it stopped," a voice from the back of the crowd shouted. Mitch knew the voice as soon as he heard it.

"Who got it stopped?" Monster looked around.

"I do. I got it stopped," Jake said patting his chest as he stepped to the front. Jake decided on his ride over that he was going to see his uncle and get to the bottom of this by hitting his gambling spot with a little plan to make his life a living hell. Mitch would pay for his betrayal. But he didn't expect the place to be so packed.

"Are you sure you wanna do that, nephew?" Mitch asked Jake. "It ain't good to bet against your own blood, youngin'!"

At that point Mitch knew that Jake knew something—about him and Kim fucking around, his affiliation with the 300, or how it was him that set her up to be killed. Either way, Jake wouldn't come in there gambling against him if he didn't think something was up.

"Yeah, I'm sure," Jake told him. "Roll the dice. Apparently blood don't mean that much nowadays, Mitch!" That was his little message to his uncle that it was on between them.

"Okay then," Mitch said. "It is what it is!" He blew on the dice and yelled, "Get 'em bitches," and rolled a 4-5-6.

"Yeah, my gee," Monster yelled.

Mitch looked at Jake. "I told you! See what happens when you go against the grain!"

"Yeah, I hear you talking, but I got more money in the bag, old man!"

All you heard was a bunch of oooohhhhs and aaaahhhs in the background. This was real dough they were playing with. With all these stories circulating around about Mr. Invincible—especially the latest one from Sparky—for him to show up out of nowhere in his uncle's gambling spot betting against him was some real hood shit. Everyone in the spot felt something was going to pop off and they were right. And it wouldn't be long. Even Monster was trying to figure out why Jake, the nephew Mitch spoke so highly about, had come out of nowhere to try to take money from his uncle.

Not getting too caught up in his thought, Monster yelled, "A hundred eighty thousand in the bank. Ten thousand and better bets."

Jake said, "I got it stopped. Roll the dice, old man."

The spot got so quiet when Jake said that the second time, you could hear a mouse pissin' on cotton. It was so intense that no one in the room moved.

"You sure you wanna do that, young blood?" Mitch asked.

"Yeah, I'm sure," Jake said smoothly. "*Are you sure* is the question. Are you really, *really* sure that I'm the one to go against?"

Mitch knew Jake wasn't talking about the dice or the money. As wrong as he was for double-crossing his nephew (he knew

he deserved death for crossing a real dude), something about
Jake's cockiness and attitude made him real upset. Maybe his
nephew's bad attitude was the reason Mitch fucked Kim or Kim
fucked Mitch in the first place. Maybe that's why Jake's own girl
didn't invite him to be part of the crew. He definitely should've
been at the card game—probably more than Kim—but he hadn't
been because he was a selfish arrogant prick. Jake had a chip
on his shoulder. He thought he was so tough. Mitch never realized it before but he wanted his nephew dead.

Mitch told himself, *fuck him,* as he blew on the dice. "Get
'em bitches!" He rolled a 4-4-5.

"Five the point," Monster stated. Jake picked up the dice,
shook them in his hand as hard as he could for about ten seconds, then he let them go. He rolled 4-5-6 and the whole place
erupted. Jake didn't crack a smile. He looked at Mitch, and
Monster slid over the $180,000, which Jake put right in his bag.

Monster, tight as hell said, "All you sweaters that ain't betters need to get the fuck out the joint!"

"My bank now," Jake said. Then he saw someone out the
corner of his eye. A face he wouldn't and couldn't forget. One of
the dudes who had robbed his store was standing there talking
to the Calvin brothers, two dudes Jake wouldn't trust any further than he could throw them. He didn't want to be too obvi-
ous that he had spotted them, so he kept it moving.

"Two hundred thousand in the bank," Jake said. "Ten thousand or better to play and if your money ain't on the floor, it
ain't a bet!"

"I'm down a buck," Mitch said, throwing ten-thousand-
dollar stacks down.

"Anybody else down?" Jake asked.

"Yeah, I got the other buck," Monster answered. "Shoot the dice, nigga! It's stopped."

Jake looked at Monster and said, "If the money ain't on the floor, it ain't a bet, ya heard!"

"Nigga you in my place," Monster told Jake.

"Main man, I'm in Mitch's place and I rolled c-low. Ten thou or better and if the money ain't on the floor it ain't a bet. Now if you down a buck put it on the floor or fall back, main man. I came here to get money not fuck around." Then he asked Mitch, "This how you do in here, Unc? Have your goon try to strong-arm the game?"

"Yo, watch your mouth before you lose a couple of your fucking teeth, nigga," Monster said, really trying to get under Jake's skin.

Mitch told Monster to take it easy. "Don't worry about it." Then he looked at Jake and said, "Don't worry about nothing. You know how this gambling shit go, a bunch of talk. Nothing to worry about, though."

Jake looked at Mitch and snickered. "I ain't worried. See no reason to be. We family, right?" Then Jake asked, "Anyone else down?"

"Yeah, I'm down fifty." It was one of the Calvin brothers who chimed in, strolled over, and threw his money on the floor. Jake looked up to see where the other brother went but he was gone. The cat that had participated in robbing his store was still across the room.

Jake yelled, "Fifty left in, who got it?"

The other Calvin brother, who Jake hadn't spotted, walked over and said, "Me," and threw his money down.

"Okay, this is the big one," Jake whispered to himself. He

shook the dice as hard as he could for ten seconds, then threw the dice. First number came up. It was a 1. Second number came up. It was a 2. The third die just kept spinning. Mitch and the Calvin brothers were hoping for a 3, but a 4 registered. Jake picked them up and shook the dice again, this time for twenty seconds. When he let them go, 4-5-6 came up. With the grace and speed of a cheetah he scooped the money off the floor and put it in his bag—at the same moment, he withdrew the gun at his waist. Without hesitating, he put the nozzle to Mitch's fore-head and threw his book bag over his shoulder. This move had Mitch, Monster, the Calvin brothers, and the whole spot fucked up. It was so unexpected.

Jake said, "Mitch, turn the fuck around and walk toward the door, motherfucker." He looked at Monster and the Calvin brothers. "Try it if you want, motherfuckers. I can't wait to lay one of you down!" As he was talking, Jake reached for the other gun at his waist, pulled it out, and waved it around the room. "Everybody get the fuck down before I start shooting!"

Those close to the door and away from Jake ran out. Those within his range did exactly what he said. The advantage that Jake had over most everyone in the room was that he had nothing to lose. He did not give a fuck. Neither Mitch nor the Calvin brothers could have afforded to pull a move like that on Jake; it would have made them too hot, they'd have to be really stupid to risk their freedom like that. Even Monster couldn't see that one coming. He pulled out his .357, but Mitch told him to put it down.

"Yo, Jake, it ain't that serious!" Monster said, putting his gun away. "What the fuck are you doing? That's your uncle!"

Jake just shot him a wicked look. Mitch thought about spin-nin' around and trying to disarm his nephew.

As if Jake could read his thought, he said, "Go 'head, Mitch! Try and see if you still got it and get your brains all over the fucking place."

"What the fuck are you doing, Jake? Why me? What's going on? First, you come in to gamble against me, now this?"

"Mitch, shut the fuck up and stop acting stupid!" Jake stopped where the robber of his store was on the floor. "Yo, you dickhead, who sent you to rob my store? Did you think I didn't recognize you or did you just think I was pussy?"

"Yo, fam, I didn't rob your shit," the man on the floor said in his defense.

"Now I'm getting tight! Dickhead, I remember you and I want an answer!"

"Yo, I didn't rob your shit!" Dude held fast.

"Okay," Jake said. "Stand up!"

"Yo, chill, I told you I didn't rob your shit!"

"Stand the fuck up!"

"Don't do this, man, you got me mixed up."

"Fuck you, nigga!" BOOM BOOM BOOM. Jake tore him up and walked out the room.

"Let's go, Uncle. We got family business to discuss."

Soon as they stepped out the door Jake kicked Mitch in his ass, causing him to fall to the concrete.

"What the fuck are you doing, Jake? Why me?"

"Hold on, Uncle. Watch this!" Jake pulled a matchbook out of his pocket, struck one, and threw it against the front door of the spot. "Get a good look at that, Unc!" POOOFFFFF! A big flame ignited.

"Hey, Mitch, I squeezed gas on the front of the building. I had a feeling I would be in a hurry out the front and I didn't want anyone behind me. Don't worry, everyone will make it out the back nice and safe, but it's definitely a wrap for your spot! Now go to the fucking car I got parked right there and hop in the driver's seat! We gotta have a talk. I'm gonna hop in the back in case you ain't talking right!"

"Yo, Jake, you're buggin'! You gotta slow down! This is me. At least give me the benefit of the doubt. I'm your uncle. I raised you. What the fuck! Not my bum-ass crackhead brother, but me. I was always there for you and this is how you repay me?"

"Why did you fuck Kim, Mitch? Out of everyone in the world you had to fuck my girl?"

"I'm not going to lie to you, boy. I slept with her, but you shouldn't kill your family over no bitch! That ain't good family principles nor street principles. You didn't know that girl like you think you did. She was pure evil!"

"So did you have something to do with her death, Mitch?"

"Yes I did, Jake. If I didn't kill her you wouldn't have made it. How do you think those people kept finding you? It was her."

"Drive faster, Mitch, and tell me more before I lose it and blow your brains out."

"Fuck it! Blow my brains out, nigga, but you better think long and hard, Jake! If I wanted you dead I could have did it myself when you were in your deep sleep. Your girl Kim is the one who had you set up."

"That bitch could have killed me in my sleep, too, Mitch! So why didn't she? She even had a gun in her bag. Why didn't she shoot me?"

"Because she was given different orders. Mr. Albert Murphy wants you to die at his hands. He wants to witness your death."

"Now we getting places, Mitch! I like when you talk to me! So is this Mr. Albert Murphy the brother of Phat Murphy? Mitch, that's who wants me dead?"

"No, Jake, Albert is Phat's father. The Calvin brothers are his brothers or half brothers. All I know is Albert considers the Calvins his sons and all three of them are pretty pissed you killed Phat."

"Listen here, Mitch! First of all, I'm glad that disgusting pig is dead and I wouldn't change that for the world! Second of all, it was Phil who killed him. Not that it matters because I would have killed him anyway."

"Well then, Jake, I guess you can understand why Phil set you up to make it look like you spazzed out for nothing. He was just trying to save his own hide, which is understandable due to the circumstances."

"Yeah, I guess so, but, um, what part did you play in this, Mitch? In which other way besides fucking my girl and not letting me know who wants me dead did you do me dirty? Who's behind the 300 Crew?"

"Phil, me, and Frazier," Mitch admitted. He had nothing to lose.

"Hold up, Frazier the CO?" Jake asked.

"That's the one," Mitch answered.

"Go on," Jake told him.

Mitch kept going. "Plus Kim, Albert Murphy, and the Calvin brothers."

Jake's mind was spinning. "So it was Frazier dropping them letters on my bed? I thought you said this Albert cat wanted me to die at his hands?"

"He does, Jake. He turned himself in on some parking tickets and had his lawyer check him straight into PC. They had hopes that the letters would make you check into PC but they didn't. Phil went left on his own with the karate guy that put you in the coma. Everybody thought he did it because you was fucking M.B. and the wire was out that she was pregnant. Now I know why he wanted you dead so bad. You had the DL on him. Neither me nor Kim was in on the shit Phil did. She really wanted to keep it moving with you when you got out of the hospital and called her, but Phil got wind of that shit and told Albert. When they got to Kim they let her know it was you or her mom and then they told me the same. It's me or you. When you had Kim call me all I had to do was go to you and leave you the Caddy. They put a tracking device in the car to be able to find you wherever you went."

"How could you sell out your own blood like that, Mitch? You raised me like a son for years. I idolized you for the longest! I put in work with you when I was young and you sell me out for some organization? Are you that scared of Albert Murphy and his sons? Or is the money so good that you just don't give a fuck about anybody?" The car sped up. "Mitch, are you trying to scare me by speeding up 'cause you're doing about eighty miles per hour and we ain't even on the highway yet."

"Listen to me, Jake, I can understand you being upset and wanting to kill me but you don't know these dudes and what they're capable of doing. They even kill friends! If I didn't kill

Kim she would have set you up again. I could have got you that night but I kept going. I was hoping you would keep going, too. I spared you twice. All I'm asking is that you spare me."

"You didn't spare me and Kim didn't spare me. You tried to set me up! If Murphy's family didn't have such a grudge, you probably would have did it yourself."

"I was ordered to hurt you and not kill you."

"Mitch, you're lying about some things and telling the truth about some things. But I'm getting tired of all this. Pull over and get the fuck out the car! I'm gonna spare you, nigga, cause you my blood!"

"Jake, I know you're lying. You're gonna shoot me."

"I said pull the fuck over, Mitch, and get the fuck out or I might change my mind about killing you!"

Mitch stopped the car and got out. Jake let him walk a few feet, then got out behind him. "You know you should have killed me, Unc, and you're lying about Mr. Albert wanting to kill me himself. There was only one hit man when it was me and Nine-One, and I killed him personally. After Kim and I left the hospital, it was two shooters and they both got arrested. You should have just told the truth and said you did me dirty and you don't know why, but you tried to lie to me instead. You said Kim was giving up our locations but you set me up with your car with the tracking device. Your stories aren't adding up!"

"What are you gonna do, nephew?"

Jake pulled a gun off his waist, put it on the ground, and kicked it to his uncle. "I'm gonna give you a chance to pick that gun up and defend yourself."

"That's mighty kind of ya, youngin'! You want me to reach

for it so you'll have an excuse to shoot me. You want to be able
to justify killing your blood. Well, Jake, I won't do it! You want
to shoot me, then shoot."

"Okay, then have it your way." Jake squeezed the trigger on
the 9mm. The first bullet smashed directly into Mitch's face.
Jake squeezed again. The second bullet hit the same spot the
first one had. Then Jake let his whole clip off into Mitch's face.
After he was dead, Jake wished Mitch to rot in hell. Jake had
enough info to handle his business. He knew exactly who
wanted to kill him and why. There was no more mystery. As far
as his life went, he knew it was over. He would definitely be
wanted for homicide, and more than one. There was no turn-
ing back. He wasn't going to jail for the rest of his life. He made
up his mind. He would kill every one of his enemies then flee
somewhere off the radar or he would die on the streets.

Jake ran back to his car and drove off. He knew he would
have to get rid of it soon and he knew he needed a place to lay
his head. He had enough money to breeze right then and there
but he was beyond the point of no return. He wanted to kill for
all the bullshit they put him through. His next mission would
be to find out where he could locate Albert Murphy and the
Calvin brothers.

THE RIGHT SIDE

The Calvin brothers stopped by Albert Murphy's house, who happened to be resting, but was happy with the news they brought him. Albert said to the Calvin brothers, "I was tired of Mitch anyway! That was a man of many games. Jake did us a favor! You can't trust a man who would turn on his own family. Notice how we keep getting smaller and smaller. I hate this Jake, but I'm glad he did what he did because now he's wanted for Mitch's murder. So we will get to this guy one way or the other. Whether we get him first or the law does, one thing is for sure: We got him right were we want him."

The eldest Calvin brother spoke. "Listen, Pops, I think you should leave town for a while until we put him down or until the cops nab this guy! He's a loose cannon, he'll try anything!

You have to be careful with guys like that. Our best bet is to get you outta here."

"Fuck no, boys," Albert said. "I'm not running or hiding from this prick! He is the one that needs to be worried. Maybe he will do us a favor and kill Phil, too. Then all we got left is Frazier to take care of. That will be easy! Then the whole house is cleaned. We'll have a clean slate. But, I couldn't imagine re-locating for any one man, especially some street punk! Phil was thinking of snatching his child's mother and his baby. I told him 'No, it's not the time now.' I should have had you boys murder him and that bitch and his child that night!"

The younger Calvin brother said, "We would have, but our window of time before the police came was too short. Besides, you ordered no more killing of innocent people. No more women or children. You said it was bad for the business. But if you let us go back to our old ways we can handle this thing much faster."

"Well, women and kids are a no-go for now. Things are get-ting too hot! If any women or kids die now, we won't be able to get money until a lot of people are locked up and we don't need our money to slow down. So we gonna play it cool until this Jake character comes back. How long can he last out there?"

―――――

Jake was wondering the same thing. He decided against getting a room. He would stay on the streets tonight and think out how he was going to get to his enemies. He knew he had to get to Phil in order to find out about the rest of their gang.

Jake ditched M.B.'s rental car and went and bought an all black '98 Crown Vic the next morning. That would be his home for a few weeks. He threw the dealer four gees to rock with his plates for a month. The car cost him six thousand so the dealer was really coming up. Jake figured his first move could be his last so he had to have his plan down to a tee. Frazier would be the easy one to get, so Jake staked out the jail in his Crown Vic.

It took Frazier two days to come out but it was just in time. Jake was tired of sitting in the car. He was tired of shitting and eating in the doughnut shop down the block and he needed a shower.

Frazier drove a black Tahoe, looked like a 2007. Jake had to laugh to himself when he stopped in the same doughnut shop Jake had been shitting and eating in for the past forty-eight hours. Frazier got a few things and, to Jake's surprise, he got in the car and drove less than five blocks before pulling into a driveway. Jake didn't waste any time. He pulled into the driveway with him. Frazier wasn't paying attention and when he did look up it was too late. Jake was out the car with his gun out.

"What the fuck are you doing here, Jake?" Frazier asked.

"What the fuck does it look like I'm doing, Frazier? I'm standing in your driveway with a gun and you know goddamn well what I'm doing here! I'm here to do what you attempted to do to me."

"Listen, Jake, you don't want to do that. It ain't worth it!" Jake walked Frazier to the porch.

"Shut the fuck up and open the door, Frazier! I got some things to ask you. Answer right and you might live to see tomorrow."

Frazier opened the door and sat down at the kitchen table cool as cucumber. "So, what is it you want to know, Jake?"

"Where's Murphy and the Calvin brothers? I'm pretty sure

you know I killed my uncle so you should know I'll have no problem putting your brains all over your table and floor if you don't answer me!"

"Yeah, I know what you're capable of, Jake. What's your point?"

"Frazier, was that you who wrote those letters?"

"Yeah, it was me and yeah, I was doing it for Albert Murphy, and it was business. I actually like you, Jake! I was just doing my job as far as the letters were concerned. That shit that happened to you with Franklin Butler, I had nothing to do with."

"Let me ask you something else, Frazier. Was that you I was on the phone with at my child's mother's house?"

"No, I wasn't on the phone with you and no I wasn't there at all." Frazier was lying. "Listen to me, Jake, you might have got to Mitch and myself but you don't have a chance with Murphy and the Calvin brothers!"

"Why not, Frazier? Who the fuck are they?" Before he could answer, Jake said, "You know what? I'm tired of fucking around with you, Frazier. I'm going to make you pay for playing a part in this."

Jake heard the front door open and turned his head for a second. Frazier used the distraction to draw a gun from his waistline and point back at Jake.

"Baby, you home?" a female voice called out. Jake knew that voice and when Brenda the nurse walked into the kitchen, the last thing she expected to see was Jake and her boyfriend holding guns at each other. She hadn't seen or heard anything about him since the hospital. In a panicked voice she asked, "What's going on? Why are you here, Mr. Billings?"

"Not to hurt you, miss. I'm here for answers."

"What kind of answers require you both pointing guns in my kitchen?"

"Ask him."

Frazier finally spoke up. "Listen to me, Jake, I don't know where Albert, the Calvin brothers, or Phil live. I don't know how to find them unless they call me and wanna meet up. The info you came over here to get, I ain't got it. So what you wanna do?"

Brenda asked Jake and Frazier, "Can y'all please put the guns down?"

"I don't think I can do that, Brenda. Your boyfriend and his crew want me dead. I kinda have no choice but to be in your kitchen with a gun drawn! What a small fucking world! One of you tried to get me killed and the other tried to help me live. Ain't that some shit you only see in the movies?"

"Brenda, get outta the kitchen," Frazier told her, never letting his eyes off Jake.

"Yeah, Brenda, get the fuck outta here," Jake joined in.

"I'm not going nowhere! Y'all want to shoot? Shoot with me right here, then." She walked directly into their line of fire. "This is my home and there will be no shooting in it! Frazier, you are my man and stay here time to time so I'm asking you to respect me. Mr. Billings, I tried my best to help you, clean you, and talk to you when you was in that coma. So I'm asking you to respect my home. Put your gun down and leave please!"

Jake didn't say a word. He kept his gun on Frazier and backed out the door. He would respect the lady's wishes. As he was driving, weighing his odds of making it, Jake wasn't pleased with himself. He should have been able to finish Frazier despite that nurse. That opportunity might not present itself again. Frazier would definitely be on point. He thought about laying Brenda down, too, but that would have been plain old foul. He was a better man than that, but for how long? He had thoughts to lay low for a while, being he had fumbled twice. Once with Phil and his attacker and now with Frazier. As he drove around thinking about his next move, Jake saw sirens flash in his rearview mirror. There was no way he could outrun them in the vehicle he was in, and he didn't want to shoot it out with them right then and there. Jake pulled over, put his gun in his waist, and rolled the window down. He saw only one officer in his rearview mirror.

"Good evening, sir. License and registration, please."

"What's the problem officer?"

"Your taillight is out, sir. License and registration, please."

Jake had no choice but to shoot the officer. *Fuck it,* he thought. Maybe he had one other option.

"Officer, my papers are in my bag. Do you mind if I get them?"

"Go ahead but be slow, please, sir."

"Okay, here we go. Here's my license and here's my registration." Jake put twenty thousand dollars on the dashboard, then another twenty thousand. And there's my insurance."

As the bright-eyed officer quickly took the money, he told Jake, "Your papers look straight to me, sir! I would get that taillight fixed, though."

"Thanks officer! I'll make sure I take care of that ASAP." Jake said to himself, "I can't afford for no shit like that to happen again. Freedom is priceless and I ain't acting like it is." Jake found a quiet dark block with no activity and parked the Crown Vic. He was tired and needed to figure out what to do next. He was going to sneak into his condo and see what Kim had laying around. He thought it was funny how when a hood nigga die they (society) act like that shit don't even matter.

After finding nothing of importance in the condo, Jake decided to go back to the airport motel so he could get some good rest and a hot meal without having to worry about police. When he got to the joint, he expected to see the funny-talking old man he could barely understand, but the place was empty. Jake still had his room key in his bag and he still had money on the room so he was straight. He went into his room, which they had cleaned up pretty good, turned on the television, and laid down. He put on the local news, but heard no mention of the two killings nor anything about him being a wanted man.

Jake fell asleep and woke up to a knock on the door. It wasn't the funny-talking clerk he expected, but Jake assumed this lady was his wife.

"Hey sweetie! I'm sorry to wake you but I need to know if that black Crown Victoria in the parking lot is yours because if not, I have to get it towed out of here."

"Yes, ma'am, that's mine."

"You didn't have a car on the day you checked in?"

"No, ma'am, I didn't," Jake answered.

"Oh, okay. That old fool ain't losing it then. When you check in you supposed to say what you driving and he supposed to write the plate, make, and model of the car so we know it belongs to a customer, but my husband always forgets. He's a damn fool! He need to put his teeth in his mouth. Bad enough he bit the tip of his tongue off, now no one can understand a damn thing that man is saying!! You hungry, son?"

"Yeah," Jake said chuckling to himself. He thought the little lady was a trip and she looked exactly like Santa Claus's wife.

"Well come to the kitchen. I'm about to make some breakfast."

Jake went into the kitchen and saw the same people he saw on the day he checked in. Three black old-timers and two middle-aged Spanish women. He sat down and ate toast and oatmeal and drank orange juice. He couldn't help but wonder why Kim or Mitch didn't kill him when they had the chance. There were a lot of loops in both of their stories.

———————

As Jake was eating breakfast, Phil and Frank were at one of Phil's lavish pads.

"I can't fucking believe Mitch and one of the guys I hired to rob Jake's store is dead! This fucking guy is something else! This is why I have you with me, Frank. Because Murphy and his sons are slippin'! Do you know I provided them with her address, and it wasn't easy to get. I had to press the top three real estate agents I knew and spend a fortune before one of them gave me what I needed. So Jake should have been killed right along with his bitch! They had 'em the other night. They were right there, but Albert is going soft with his new policy!"

"What is his new policy, if you don't mind me asking, Phil?"

"Hell no, I don't mind you asking, Frank! His new policy is: no women or kids anymore. That will draw too much heat on us, which I agree with, but for this one case, for the life of me I can't understand why they would want to spare a cunt like that! That's why I don't trust them and I have to get them before they get me. All of these guys are the same. They use you and then try to get you a pair of cement shoes. I got a trick for these cock-suckers, though!"

"Listen, Phil, I don't know Mr. Murphy or the Calvin brothers but I'm gonna take your word on what kind of guys they are. I do know the type of shit this guy Jake is pulling is crazy and we have to be extra careful. He feels he has nothing to lose and that's gonna make him extremely hard to deal with. We don't know anything about where he is staying, who he's with, or if he has any friends with him. We have to take all of these things into consideration."

"That's why you're the man, Frank! You're tough and you're smart! You know I wouldn't know what to do without you," Phil sang out.

Frank ignored the compliment. "What's the deal with the CO? I don't hear you talk about Frazier much. You good with him?"

"Yeah, Frank, I'm cool with him! Frazier ain't stupid. I have a feeling he'll be calling to have a meeting alone with me one day."

———

Frazier was having issues of his own. Instead of breakfast, he was getting the third degree.

"Why was Jake Billings in my kitchen pointing a gun at you, talking about you wanting him dead? What is going on?" Brenda asked. "What are you doing?"

"The guy lost it, Brenda! How should I know what's going on in his head? Maybe because I was the CO on duty when he got stabbed. Some loony runs in here with a gun on me and you asking me what's going on? I'm outta here! Brenda, I really like you. We've been dating for about a year and shit been cool, but in the last two months you've been a little too clingy. I ain't into no one giving me the third degree. Fuck that! So if you wanna talk we can talk, but the third degree with the funny tone ain't gonna work!"

"Well, you can leave then, because you should understand I got the right to be upset when there are guns out in my house, Frazier!"

"You right and I'm sorry, Brenda! That shit just had me on edge. I ain't got no answers, though. I think he's just bugging because I was the man on duty when he got put in a coma. It is kinda weird that I was his CO and you was his nurse. It's a small world after all!"

"I gotta work doubles today and tomorrow at the hospital so I'm gonna stay over there, Fraze. I don't want to stay in this house right now anyway after that incident!"

"I hear you, Brenda. We can move somewhere together now. That was more than a good enough reason to get a place together."

Frazier was serious. Not only because of Jake, but he couldn't trust the remaining members in the 300 Crew.

"I'm gonna get a room somewhere tonight myself," Frazier said. "I ain't gotta go back to work for at least three more days. I'ma shoot some pool into the wee hours of the night, down a couple of cold ones, find me a good bag of weed, and call it a night. You have a good place I could go?"

"As a matter of fact I do. Me and a few nurses stayed at this cute mom-and-pop motel by the airport a few times. It ain't fancy or nothing like that, but they have some of the best steak and eggs, the rooms are clean and cheap, and the people are nice. There was this crazy old man at the front desk and we could hardly understand a word he said. His wife says he bit the tip of his tongue off and never wears his dentures, but they are the sweetest people in the world! If you decide to go, let me know. I'd rather come stay over there with you and it's not that far from the hospital."

"Sounds good to me, Brenda! I'll wait for you, drop you off at work, and you can tell me where the place is. I will get the room and whenever you finish your shift you can give me a call and I'll shoot back to get you."

Frazier wanted to chill out and settle down with Brenda and leave the 300 Crew alone, and the bullshit CO job. He knew he had enough money to just up and leave and stop fucking with the 300, but he knew he would have to hide. If you did business with Murphy and stopped, he felt he had to kill you to cover his ass. But Frazier felt if he could just play it cool, if he could just have some time . . . He knew Phil and Albert didn't really like each other and who could blame them? They were both scum-bags. One of them was going to put the other down eventually. And if Frazier had to choose one of them to ride with, he was going with Phil. Murphy was just too foul. *He would eventually find a reason to kill me,* Frazier thought. No, Frazier couldn't wait around; he had to make a move and make it soon. Frazier picked up his cell and called Phil.

Phil answered. "Hey, Fraze! What's up my man? I was just talking about you with my main man, Frank."

Frazier's tone was serious. "We need to meet up, Phil. I wanna talk to you about a few things that's kinda urgent. When can we meet?"

"Shit, we can meet now, Fraze! Come on over, lets talk over lunch."

"I don't wanna be seen going into anyplace you're known to be at. I wouldn't want our friends getting any funny ideas. So let's pick a safe spot. You know what I mean, Phil!"

"Where do you consider safe nowadays, Fraze?"

"I'm gonna call you back and let you know when I find one. I'm thinking a McDonald's or department store parking lot or a laundromat somewhere. We know our friends don't go nowhere next to one of them kinda places, you know what I mean?"

"Yeah, I get you, Fraze," Phil said. "I get you loud and clear. Well, you find a place and get back to me and I will be there."

"Hey, Phil?"

"Yeah, Fraze."

"Make sure you bring Franklin Butler with you. We're gonna need him."

"I told you," Phil said to Frank after hanging up with Frazier. "I told you that guy would be calling soon to have a meeting. He's no fool! He knows Murphy is a snake and he plans on doing us greasy. That's how he works, but boy oh boy are we gonna fuck with him!"

Frazier called Phil back and told him to meet him in a parking garage that was downtown on the rough side and be sure not to be followed. Phil and Frank hopped in a cab just to make sure no one was following them. When they got to the meeting spot, Frazier was sitting in his Tahoe and told them to hop in.

"Frank, Phil. How are you guys doing?" Frazier asked.

"Frank's fine and I'm fine. What's up, Fraze?"

"Straight up, Phil, if we don't kill Murphy he is going to kill us. Ever since Kim ran off it ain't been right. I've known Albert a long time and I've seen him kill people he claimed to love. Imagine what he will do to us! He thinks somebody's gonna talk to save their own skin. It's only me and you left, Phil. We have to watch each other's backs now."

Frazier continued. "One other thing. I'm actually lucky to be alive! Jake Billings almost put my brains on my kitchen table. My girl saved my life by making noise and then stepping into his line of fire. If she had not made noise I wouldn't have been able to draw, so I guess God was on my side."

Phil told Frazier he was glad they met, and he said it wouldn't be too long before they sat down again and figured out a way to get rid of Albert Murphy and Jake Billings.

CHAPTER 19

FOR THE PEOPLE

Jake sat in his room and watched the news. His stomach was full from all the food he'd eaten, and he was bored. He was trying his best to piece together the stories he had heard from Mitch and Kim but none of the shit made sense to him. He again felt like he was living out some kind of movie. He got who wanted him dead and why, but how his uncle and girl, the two closest people to him, were fucking around with each other and in some gang was amazing to him. Then something came on the news that damn near made Jake faint. The reporter said something about finding the body of Mitch Billings. Then they mentioned finding a federal agent's dead body in his car a few weeks prior. When they showed a picture of the agent it was Nine-One. Jake couldn't believe it. He didn't know what to think. He felt like the feds were going to kick in the door at any second.

Jake wasn't the only one shocked by the news. So were Phil, Frazier, the Calvin brothers, and Albert. They were even more shook up than Jake. A federal agent being found dead in Mitch's car was real bad news. The number one rule for the boys—even bigger than no innocents—was once they heard the feds were involved, all criminal activity had to stop. No white-collar crimes, no blue-collar crimes, no robberies, no drug deals, no nothing. They couldn't even communicate with one another. Everyone was in panic mode.

Jake had plans to wait for the wee hours of the morning and take it to the train and travel by public transportation until he got far away. He was thinking of heading to Mexico; anywhere that was far away from them bars whispering his name. He was gonna call M.B. later and say his goodbyes. He wanted to see his baby one more time if possible. He couldn't help but think about how Nine-One was a fed. *Who was he watching more, me or Kim? And if my uncle called him up, did he know he was a fed? Was Mitch a fed, too? Was Kim a fed? Maybe they didn't kill me because they're feds. Or maybe they didn't kill me because they knew the feds were watching.*

———

Albert Murphy and his sons may have been thinking that they were in trouble and that their whole world was about to be destroyed, but Phil didn't think negative. He figured there were too many other people to blame. There was no way he couldn't wiggle his way out of any legal trouble. Phil had dirt on a few important feds, too. If he had to use that trump card, he was more than prepared to do so.

Phil told Frank, "I'm actually happy because right now Albert is shitting his pants and he won't be thinking straight. It is time for us to make a plan to get rid of him. This is fucking great, Frank! I wanna celebrate."

Frank asked Phil, "You just heard federal agent and one of your partner's names in the same sentence. How could you possibly be happy?"

"Because the feds ain't shit, either, Frank! I got dirt on a few important ones and that is my get-out-of-jail-free card! That's why I'm not worried, because I'm prepared. I'm smart and I'm the fucking man on my way to running the whole entire fucking city! You should be happy, Frank, because you will be right there with me!"

"Hey, Phil, before you start celebrating, don't forget about our other problem. He is not going to disappear. We have to make him go away. You have to stay focused and stay on point!"

———————

Jake had to tell himself to calm down. He was not leaving town without killing Phil and his attacker. He could let Murphy slide but not Phil. Phil had to pay. He was the lowest motherfucker in Jake's eyes. Any man that tries to kill a man that helped him before is a lowlife. His girl was dead. He had killed his uncle. Nine-One was dead—and a fucking fed at that—and he couldn't be around his kid and M.B. He was gonna torture Phil. Jake told himself he was gonna kill him slow and enjoy it.

Jake thought his eyes were playing tricks on him. He was looking out the window and he thought he saw Frazier's truck pull into the hotel parking lot. As he looked closer, he couldn't believe it.

"Holy shit," he said to himself. "No fucking way."

As Frazier stepped out of his truck Jake was glad he had followed his instincts after seeing that shit about his uncle and about Nine-One being a fed. He made sure to park his hoopty a few blocks away from the hotel. He didn't want to attract any unnecessary heat.

Then he thought, *What if he knows I'm here and is coming for me?*

Jake discarded that thought when he saw Frazier go back to his truck and put his jacket inside and then double back to get his cigarettes out of his jacket. He was in relax mode. Jake wasn't going to let him slide this go-round. He wouldn't let this opportunity go by.

Jake got all of his things together. He wanted to leave his bag in the hoopty so he would be able to move fast after he handled his business. Jake waited in his room on edge, torn between wanting to break out and wanting to kill Frazier. He looked out often to see if Frazier went back to his car; he did after a few hours. Frazier got into his car and drove off.

Jake grabbed his bag and hit the door. He was cautious in approaching the lobby, just in case Frazier was trying to lay on him. He was prepared to get it in, and if police popped out he planned on going out in a blaze, but the lobby was dead—nothing was happening. He could hear the lady attendant who looked like Mrs. Santa Claus telling the two ladies and her husband to go and clean the room. The nice young man was coming back later. Then she noticed Jake was standing there.

"Can I help you, sweetie? You hungry or you need something?"

"No, thank you, ma'am. I just want to pay to keep my room for another week."

Jake paid his money and kicked around in the lobby. He wanted to see what room the ladies were gonna go clean. Sure as shit they went to clean the room directly across from his—Frazier's room. What more could he ask for? He wished the rooms were not on the first floor, but it was okay with him because there was minimum activity. Jake walked back to his room, slowly, looking into Frazier's room as best he could to see what the CO had going on—the answer was not much. He went into his room and sat in the chair by his door. When Frazier returned he would be able to hear him.

Hours and hours had passed. It was 11:30 at night and the hotel was silent. Jake was getting restless and impatient until he looked out the window and saw Frazier's Tahoe pull up. Jake wasn't sure but it looked like Frazier had a little buzz from how he stumbled out the car and had a wobble in his walk. Jake put his book bag on his back and waited by his door. He cocked the other 9mm he took from M.B. He had got rid of the one he used on Mitch, but he pulled out the .38 he had from Kim. He unlocked his door and opened it a little. As soon as he heard Frazier get to his door, he planned on flinging his open and giving it to Frazier.

Jake heard the footsteps get closer and closer. When Jake heard him stop at the door he flung his open to finish Frazier. Just as he was about to squeeze off both guns, he realized it wasn't Frazier. It was Brenda. Brenda, seeing the guns, screamed her lungs off.

"Aaaaagghhh!"

"Shut the fuck up," Jake said and put his guns down. He ran toward the lobby. He knew he didn't have time to spare. He would have to run up on Frazier and finish him.

Brenda trailed, yelling, "Frazier, watch out! Jake, stop! Please stop."

The moment Frazier heard the scream his gun was drawn and he was running toward the room to get Brenda. He had no idea it was Jake until he heard Brenda yell out his name. Then they were in sight of each other. Jake didn't hesitate squeezing the nine mm.

Four shots flew past Frazier, who let off two shots of his own back at Jake. He was a much better shot than Jake. The two bullets out of his glock found a home in Jake's left shoulder. They made him hit the floor and take cover behind a couch in the lobby.

"Brenda, get outta here. Go to the car," Frazier barked.

Brenda listened and ran out. She didn't want Frazier to kill Jake, but this wasn't a time for debate. Jake Billings was crazy and even she knew it. It was hard to deal with people like that. They only understood one thing: violence.

Frazier knew he'd hit Jake and yelled, "I am about to finish you off, you fucking punk." Jake was in a world of pain. He lifted his right arm above the couch and squeezed off three shots blindly, just hoping to hit Frazier.

Yelling, "Well, come on, bitch."

Nothing landed.

"Looks like it's over, Jake. You can fight, but you can't shoot," Frazier teased. "I'll see you around boy!"

Frazier wasn't a fool. He was getting out of there before one of those shots hit him directly or ricocheted off of something.

"Hold this tough guy."

Frazier let off five shots in the couch. Luckily for Jake, none of those hit him. He heard Frazier run out the door. Jake yelled out of frustration. He missed the opportunity to get Frazier again and he got two bullets in his shoulder for his failing efforts, almost losing his life. Jake got up and scurried out the door. He wished he had parked closer. He knew he had to go to the hospital for his shoulder. He was bleeding a lot and knew he stood a chance of bleeding to death. Jake made it to the car, and just in the nick of time, he heard sirens in the distance. He was pretty sure they were going to the place he just left.

Jake knew he was in a tight spot. He felt like he would die soon and his time was running out. He figured his best bet was to try to make it to the hospital the next town over. The one where Brenda worked and he had laid in for two years was out of the question. Jake pulled off in the old Crown Vic thinking of his daughter. He wished he had more time to spend with her. Jake drove a couple of blocks and remembered that his taillight was fucked up. He could see the sirens in his rearview. He knew his car wasn't the fastest, but he mashed on the gas. He put his guns on his lap. He wasn't buying his way out of this one. He was trying to think but everything was moving fast.

Jake screamed, "Aaaaaaaaahhh fuck," and slammed his fist on the wheel. The cop was right behind Jake on the loudspeaker.

"Pull over. Pull over. Pull the vehicle over."

Jake mashed on the gas harder. By this time another cop had joined the chase. Sirens were flashing and whoo-whooing. At that time, Jake didn't know what it was, but he couldn't help but to think of the words to Biggie Small's song, "Suicidal Thoughts."

When I die fuck it I wanna go to hell / 'cause I'm a piece of shit it ain't hard to fucking tell . . .

Jake saw a club and the parking lot was packed full. This might be his only chance to get away, he told himself. So he threw his bag on his shoulder, put his .38 in his pants, mashed the brakes, and jumped out and left the car in drive so that it kept rolling. He ran toward the crowd. When he got to the crowd, he fired a shot into the air causing havoc, which made people stampede out of the lot running for safety. It caused enough of a diversion to get away.

Jake tucked his gun in his pants and tried to blend with the crowd. He saw that he was passing by a familiar face he did not want to see at the moment. It was Monster, but he hadn't spotted Jake. Monster was busy trying to find his cousins. They had just came home and he wanted to make sure they were all right.

Jake heard Monster say to one of his homies: "Yo, go make sure Dollar and Lil Red a'ight, my nigga. Motherfuckers is flipping out here!"

"A'ight, Monster," the dude said.

Jake kept his gun tucked in his pants, but his hand was on the grip. Then Jake heard, "Yo, Monster, this shit is crazy, cuz."

"Word niggaz, this shit is poppin'! Who the fuck popped off out here?"

It was Dollar and Lil Red. Jake couldn't believe it.

Monster said, "I don't know, my niggaz. One of these wild-ass niggaz. They made it hot, though. Police all over this motherfucker."

Jake looked and noticed Monster was right. They had the place surrounded. Jake felt like he wasn't going to make it out and he was on the verge of passing out.

"This motherfucker got some balls coming here," Lil Red said, pointing to Jake.

Monster wanted to pull out his .357, but it was too late. Jake had his gun out pointing it at the three of them.

"What the fuck is up now, niggaz?" Jake asked. "You got a big fucking mouth, Red! You do, too, asshole!" Jake was referring to Monster.

Monster replied, "Fuck you, nigga," and reached for his gun.

Jake let all three of them have it. He emptied the rest of the 9mm on them and dropped to the ground from his loss of blood. He tried to get up and run, but his body wouldn't do what his brain was telling it to do. Jake saw police closing in, looking for who fired the last few shots off. Then he heard, "Freeze! Put it down."

Jake looked, and to his surprise the cops weren't talking to him. It was homeboy who Monster had sent to find Lil Red and Dollar. He had seen Jake pop his peeps and he drew his gun to let Jake have it. He was too slow though and didn't see the cop standing right next to him. With all the people scrambling to get out of there, all the commotion and screaming, Jake made use of the opportunity to blend in and slide off with the crowd. He managed to get out of the lot.

"Yo, J.B., get in, nigga!"

Jake thought he was bugging. It was Reggie in a gray Chevy Impala. Jake hopped in.

"Yo, J.B., what the fuck, nigga! Are you crazy? You trying to go to jail or get killed out this motherfucker? Yo, you got to slow the fuck down, son. I just seen that whole shit, nigga. You crazy!"

"Yo, Regg, I'm shot. I need to get to a hospital and not our hospital. Bring me out of town please, my gee."

"Jake, where you shot at? I seen you shoot and nobody shot back."

"I got shot before I got there, twice in the shoulder. Regg, get me out of here. I need a hospital."

Jake was tired and couldn't hold his eyes open.

"Yo, Jake, try to stay up, homie," Regg said. "It ain't good to go to sleep while you're bleeding."

"Yeah, I hear you, Regg. I'm good."

Then Jake closed his eyes and thought about his daughter.

When Jake woke up he was in a hospital bed. The last thing he remembered was Regg coming out of nowhere. Regg startled Jake.

"I see you up now, big homie. They said you was gonna make it through. They had to pull them two slugs up out you, though. How you feel, my gee?"

"Like shit, Regg, but on some real shit, I owe you. If you ain't show up when you did, I don't know what would have happened to me."

"Yo, Jake, you loose as shit you know. I seen that whole shit go down from when you pulled up with them pigs on your ass. I see why they call you Mr. Invincible. I mean I heard how you did at that dice game. They said you did some wild shit in a cab trying to kill a couple of dudes one day, but that shit I seen you pull takes the cake."

"Yo, get me outta here, Regg. Do you still got my bag?"

"Yo, Jake, chill out. We a couple of towns away. You safe and your bag is safe. I got you. I'm going to hold you down, homie."

"Listen, Regg. I'm glad you showed up when you did because I wouldn't have made it if you didn't. As a man I'm grateful for that. I want you to take half that money in the bag, but anyone around me doesn't seem to stay alive. So I would be grateful if you got me out of here and let me get your car."

Regg shook his head. "Yeah, I feel you, homie. I'm going to get you up outta here, but you could have your money, fam. I'm good. I helped you because you was in a tight spot and you a good dude. I felt you would do the same for me. As far as a motherfucker deading me I can hold my own. Worry about yourself. You the one laying in a hospital bed, not me, my gee. If you wanna buy my car off me, cool, but I don't want nothing else from you. I'm straight. You ready to move now, Jake?"

"Yeah, Regg, let's get outta here. I'm fucking paranoid. I don't want to sit still. I gotta keep moving."

Jake was getting out of bed while he was talking and removing the tape and tubes attached to his arms.

"You think you should be ripping off that IV like that, homie? You really trying to walk outta here half naked like that?" Regg asked.

"Why the fuck not? If I'm alive, this little IV ain't what's holding me up and my ass could use the air," Jake said half jokingly.

"Let's move, then."

Jake and Regg bounced out the hospital and got in Regg's car.

When they got a few miles from the hospital Regg asked, "Where you headed, Jake?"

"I have no destination. I'm gonna just keep it moving, Regg. Can't think of nothing better to do."

"Well, Jake, the car gonna cost you fifteen stacks and I'm gonna get out in a few blocks. If you need a handgun you shit out of luck, but I do keep a sawed-off twelve-gauge in the trunk and that will cost you a stack. I also got some weed in the glove box but consider that a gift on me."

Jake wasn't feeling Regg. Something wasn't right, but he couldn't pinpoint it. "What was you doing at the party, Regg? Last I remember, you weren't fucking with Dollar or Lil Red."

"If you know I don't fuck with them, Jake, then you should be able to figure out why I was there, my gee. I was gonna put that work in, but you did it for me."

Jake felt funny and knew something was wrong. His instincts were telling him not to trust Regg.

Then all of a sudden Regg pulled the car over and said to Jake, "Get out of my car."

"What you say, Regg?"

"Get the fuck out the car and leave your bag of money, Jake, before it happens to you."

"What's the matter, Regg, I offered you half of the shit!"

"If you stay in this car with me I might be the one to have to kill you."

"Fuck you talking about, Regg?"

"I'm talking about taking your shit. Now get the fuck out before you lose your life," Regg said while putting his pistol to Jake's head, forcing him out of the car. "I'll leave you with a couple of stacks, though. I'm sorry, Jake, but you know how this shit be. I just got home. And I'm used to having cash. You know how we do for this money. When you see a come up you got to take it. I ain't tryin' to shit on you, I just need that paper."

"You sure that's what you wanna do, Regg?"

"I don't want to do it, but you know how this shit is."

He threw Jake about fifty thousand out of the bag and left him standing on the street.

CHAPTER 20

BACK TO THE BEAST

Jake couldn't believe Regg robbed him and left him half naked on the road. "At least I'm alive! Thank GOD," Jake said to himself. He found a plastic ShopRite bag to put the money in and walked a few blocks. He saw a yellow cab just sitting there and hopped in.

"Where you headed to, buddy?" the driver asked.

Jake realized he had no place to go and no one to turn to. "To be honest with you, my man, I don't know! Just take this." Jake handed him two hundred dollars. "And drive. Let me know when that runs out."

"You all right, young man? I see you just got out of the hospital. Where's your clothes at?" the driver asked with a curious look on his face.

Jake answered, "Well, my man, no I'm not all right, and it's a long story."

"Well, you'll have plenty of time to tell it."

Jake looked up and the cab driver pulled his chain badge out of his shirt and his gun from his waist. He got on a walkie-talkie. "It's him! It's him! I got him!"

"Damn," was all Jake could utter. Then he just closed his eyes. He knew it was over. He was on his way back to jail . . .

As he walked into work, Frazier couldn't believe who he saw getting processed. He couldn't resist the temptation to go over and talk to him. "I guess you're back here with me now. I'm gonna make sure you have a pleasant stay, Jake."

"Fuck you, Frazier! You lucky I didn't blow your fucking head off!"

"You're a bum shot, Jake! You know damn well you're the lucky one to be alive, but I'm going to see what I can do to change that. I'll be back, Jake, don't you go nowhere," Frazier said jokingly.

Jake got processed and sent to a cell, which took a total of eight hours. He knew they was trying to bust his balls with the bullpen therapy. Jake wondered what plans Frazier had for him, but he came to a conclusion to just fall back and let whatever was going to happen, happen. He was glad he was in a cell and not a dorm. The pressure of having to watch his back from all angles 24/7 would have made him flip. Jake knew that by this hour the whole jail knew he was back. Even though a couple of years had passed, it was the same grime balls and wild motherfuckers running around. Jake overheard some bum-ass dudes in the bullpen talking about how you can do some of your state bid right there in the local jail.

He got a good night's sleep despite being in jail. He was tired. He had been ripping and running and his body had been through a lot. It was morning and Jake was in the part of the jail where they held the hard-core criminals and dudes going to the feds. It was a more laid-back atmosphere: instead of roaming around free in the dorms, he was in a cell block where he was locked down twenty-three hours a day, which meant he only got one hour of rec.

When the time for rec came, Jake went to the yard to see what was popping; to find out who was doing what in the joint. He knew who was behind the 300 Crew and he knew he wouldn't be receiving any mystery letters. Jake knew the talk of him poppin' Lil Red, Dollar, Monster, and Mitch was all over the jail, so he wanted to find out who he was gonna have a problem with right away. As Jake got to the yard he saw a few familiar faces but he saw no force to be reckoned with. He saw Cory and Ike who seemed to have taken the place of Dollar and Lil Red. Everything else seemed to be running the same.

Jake figured it was Frazier who manipulated the 300 to work in the joint. He picked who he could use and anyone he couldn't he had his crew put pressure on; his plan was excellent.

Jake looked up and saw Frazier walking toward him as he was spinning the yard (walking around the track). "Can I talk to you, Jake?" Frazier asked.

"Your house, not mine," Jake answered as he stopped to hear what he was gonna say.

"Listen to me, Jake! I'm willing to put our recent history behind us because I can understand why you was upset. Shit, if I was you I would have did the same thing. I'm not trying to make your time any harder while you're here. That shit I said in bookings, I was fucking around with you."

"Okay, Frazier, I can go with that! I don't want no problems," Jake stated and stuck his right hand out for Frazier to shake. Frazier reached for Jake's hand. Jake had no intentions of letting Frazier slide. He was sizing him up. Frazier was just about the same height as Jake but he weighed about thirty pounds more. He looked like the kind of black man you didn't want to tussle with, like a diesel James Evans. You could tell he worked out a lot. His traps and arms made his shirts fit him tight. When Frazier's hand got in Jake's grip, Jake already knew what he was gonna do.

Jake punched him in the throat with his left hand while holding Frazier's right hand as hard as he could. The blow instantly caused Frazier to buckle and drop to his knees. He couldn't breathe. Then Jake pulled Frazier's face down, smashing his knee into Frazier's nose as hard as he could. Then he spun his neck around in a sharp 360-degree motion causing Frazier's neck to snap, killing him instantly.

Jake kept moving as Frazier lay dead on the ground. He was waiting for the turtle squad. He knew they were coming, and he knew they were going to break him up, if not kill him, but for some reason he heard no alarm sound off. He heard no one demand for him or the whole yard to lay down. It was as if the other two corrections officers didn't see what happened. They didn't.

Jake knew the yard had cameras posted on it. One way or the other they would know he did it. He didn't even give a fuck.

With Frazier dead, at least his life would feel a little less threatened.

Inmates yelling, "Yo, hit the wall. Get your back against something," was all Jake heard. He didn't know who said it but when he looked up he saw why they said it. The turtle squad was pointing at him and coming for him suited up like they were going to war—in all black with helmets, shields, and batons. Jake knew he didn't have a chance against twenty suited-up men with weapons, so he tried to get his back against the wall.

All he could remember was the first blow to his head. After that he went blank and woke up in the prison hospital ward. Jake had a tremendous headache but the rest of his body felt pretty fine—just a little soreness where he'd been shot in his leg and in his shoulder. That hand of his, the one the doctors said would never move again, wasn't moving now . . . but that was because he was cuffed to the bed.

SMART MEN

"Frank, can you fucking believe this shit? Frazier is dead! That motherfucking Jake killed him! Broke his neck with his bare hands. Frazier is a big guy! Shit, Frank, you're a master of the martial arts. How dangerous is that motherfucker if he can break another grown man's neck with his bare hands? I'm sure glad that bastard is behind bars. He won't be coming out anytime soon, but he also destroyed our jail money. There's nobody to run that part of the show anymore."

Frank was tired and looked it. He couldn't take Phil's ways anymore and told him. "I don't mean to burst your bubble, Phil, but don't you think it's time to call it quits? It's over for your Crew. It's only you and Albert Murphy and the Calvin brothers left, and you and Albert don't like or trust each other.

So why still do business with him? That makes no sense! You should know when to call it quits, especially if the feds are in the picture! To be real with you, Phil, since Jake is locked up, you don't need me anymore. I'm getting too old and I have no interest in getting involved with the shit you are doing. So after today you're gonna have to find somebody else to watch your back. I'm getting outta here. I'm moving far away."

"So that's it, Frank, it's over just like that? You're leaving me?"

"You don't need me anymore, Phil! I suggest you think about relocating. Your partners aren't the kind of guys I would stay in business with. Phil, I really like you but I don't want to be part of what you're doing. The money is good, but you got to know when to call it quits. Your track record as a lawyer is incredible! You could go to any state anywhere and live life like a king. As for me, I have to appreciate my second chance. I can't afford to keep throwing rocks at the pen. Shit is bigger than that. I'm trying to have peace of mind at the end of the day."

"Yeah, I hear you talking, Frank. It makes a lot of sense, the things you're saying, but I'm the kind of guy that wants it all. Maybe I'm greedy, maybe crazy, or both. I'm going to relocate, but when I do, wherever I go, I'm going to do the same thing. You know why, Frank?"

"No, tell me why, Phil."

"Because I can! I'm that fucking smart and that powerful! You know whoever crosses me ends up regretting it and right now I'm feeling you're crossing me, Frank!"

"Is that supposed to be a threat, Phil? If it is, I can kill you right fucking now with my bare hands since you seem to be so amazed by that," Frank warned his former boss.

"I'm just fucking with you, Frank, because I'm sad and hurt you ain't gonna be here no more! I had big plans for us," Phil said, realizing that Frank could do exactly what he just said he could. "I apologize, Frank! That was uncalled for. You have been a true friend and you saved my life before. I wish you the best."

"I wish you the same, Phil. I hope everything works out for you!" He shook Phil's hand and left his office.

Frank was going to head home, pack a small bag, and hit the road. He didn't have much in his apartment. He only had a bed, a television, and a radio. Other than that, he had always been with Phil. He knew he wanted to relocate so he never bothered with hooking the place up. He had a decent amount of money stashed in a storage room more than two hours away. He kept a half a mil sewed up in some bullshit furniture. It was more than enough for a man like him. Frank got to his apartment, hopped in the shower, then made himself a bite to eat. While he was getting dressed, he looked out of his window and spotted a black Corvette parked on the corner. Albert Murphy's men.

Frank wondered what Phil had done. Did he call Albert and tell him some bullshit? It didn't matter. He had planned for this to happen. He lived on the top floor of his building, which was six stories high. He picked that neighborhood because of all the attached rooftops. It made for an easy getaway for times like these. He had nothing of value in his place so he could up and bounce whenever.

Frank grabbed his vest and threw it on. He added a .40 cal with an extended clip (and a few extra clips for good measure) and a short Ginsu knife that was already in its sheath. He slipped into the hallway and looked around. No one was there. He hit the exit and slammed the door behind him. One flight of steps and he was on the roof. Frank peeked over the edge; the Corvette was still there and whoever was in it had gotten out and was walking into the building. It was the Calvin brothers. Frank decided to move. He began running the rooftops. He knew the roofs stayed attached for at least two blocks. He ran the distance and climbed down a fire escape. He was so prepared for this situation that he had purchased himself an all black Mustang, which he left sitting in a parking lot right across the street from the fire escape. He gave the attendant his ticket, which he always kept in his wallet, then pulled out of the parking lot smooth.

Frank couldn't believe how stupid Phil was. He was an easy guy to kill and so was the whole Crew as far as Frank was concerned. Everybody was hittable. Since no one knew what he was driving, he decided to spin a few blocks back and see if the Calvin brothers were still there. He looped around and saw that the Corvette had pulled off. Frank decided to give Phil a call. When Phil didn't pick up, Frank knew he was a coward and was behind the brothers showing up at his place. Frank would make it real for Phil and Albert. He wasn't the one for them to be fucking around with. He could finish Phil anytime he chose.

Frank knew all of Phil's patterns. He was loose and reckless. Albert Murphy was the exact opposite. He was tight and pinpoint accurate. But Frank knew if he followed the Calvin brothers he could find out where Albert was.

Phil talked so much, and Frank had picked up on the fact that the Calvin brothers liked to gamble. It wouldn't be too hard to find them. Most likely they would be in Monster's new spot. After Mitch was murdered, Monster opened up a bar/gambling spot of his own. To keep it funky, he named it after Mitch. That's where all the hustlers and gamblers met up. The Calvin brothers were sure to show up. He had the advantage because they had no idea that he was coming for them.

———

Monster and Lil Red were sitting in Red's car in front of Monster's crib reminiscing over Dollar and how the funeral was fly and geed up. When Jake shot the three of them, Dollar caught the short end of the stick. He got hit in the heart and was dead before the ambulance even got there. Monster and Lil Red were both hit. Monster in the shoulder, and Lil Red in the right side of his chest.

"I swear to you, Monster, I'm gon have niggaz finish that kid. I already know Ike and Cory is plottin'. I already sent the kite. Whoever puts that boy down, family is straight."

"I hope so, Red, because he ain't no slouch! I hope niggaz ain't scared of him. The nigga snapped a CO's neck with his bare hands in the yard, first day in. You know niggaz is gonna respect that shit. He might have a li'l army of his own by now."

"Fuck that nigga, Monster! Yeah, he get it in. I give him that, but his day is coming! Everybody think this nigga is something special 'cause he put work in after waking up from a coma, but I say the nigga is just lucky! I almost wish I was in jail so I could kill that bastard myself!"

"Shhhiiittt! I don't do them jails," Monster replied. "Too much shit to do on the outside for a player like me to be sitting on the inside. As long as there is money on his head, the job will get done so don't even sweat it, cuz! I know one thing, when we get in my spot tonight, I'm getting fucked up after I trim all of them motherfuckers' pockets. You feel me?"

"Yeah, I feel you, cuz, but I just don't feel right without my brother around. I'm going to lay low in the crib with a shorty or something. I ain't in no mood to be around nobody and I don't feel like gambling. I'll fuck around and kill a motherfucker for saying some dumb shit or just losing a roll!"

"I hear you, fam." Monster understood.

"We gonna get that boy washed up, that's my word," Red reiterated.

"Yo, I'ma catch you tomorrow then, fam," Monster said. "I got to go handle a meeting with some lawyer Mitch used to fuck with. The same one that be with the karate dude, Frank."

"Yeah, I heard that. You know what's funny? The karate dude came to us offering to do the job on Jake while we was inside like he needed sneakers and bitches. He was looking to be hooked up. That nigga was fronting all the time! I bet you he was doing that shit for somebody else; probably that lawyer! You better watch that shit, fam! It always be them motherfucking so-called legal working dudes that be the lowest of them all! Be careful, my gee! I'll get up with you tomorrow," Lil Red told Monster and dapped him up. He pulled off and Monster went in his crib.

CHAPTER 22

SMALL WORLD

Monster's spot was packed. Hood stars from everywhere were there to drink, listen to the music, bag a honey, or straight up get their gamble on.

"Yo, Monster! This a nice place! You got yourself a real classy joint," Regg told him.

"Good looking, Regg! Glad to have you here! I will be even gladder when I have all your money," Monster joked and gave Regg a dap. Monster saw the Calvin brothers and nodded "What up" to them. They did the same in return. To his surprise, his cuz Lil Red had just walked in the place, even though he said he was staying home.

Monster announced, "The c-low game started in the back. Betters not sweaters come check the action."

As soon as the game started, there was tension in the air so thick you could cut it with a knife. Everybody knew Regg and Lil Red didn't like each other. Neither one of them said a word to the other. Regg was keeping it cool out of respect. He didn't want Lil Red dead, plus his brother just died. But he wouldn't mind squaring up with him. To him, Red talked too much for a dude 5' 7" and 185 pounds. Regg wanted to knock him out 'cause he believed that Red actually thought he could beat him. Regg was 210, 6' 1", and good with his hands.

"It's my bank," one of the Calvin brothers said. "I won the peewee and it's fifty thousand in it. Ten thou and better is a go."

"I'm down twenty thousand," Monster said.

"I'm down twenty myself." Lil Red dropped his money.

"I got the ends," Regg said last.

Everybody else fell back. A lot of dudes came to gamble but the stakes were too high. You really had to have some paper to be gambling away ten thousand dollars. There was a lot of hustlers in the joint but they wasn't on that level.

"Yo, no disrespect but we don't need bystanders! If you ain't betting, go get you a drink or talk to a broad or some shit. Don't be over here waiting and sweating on other niggaz' paper," Monster yelled out. Mad motherfuckers got the drift. It was a couple of motherfuckers mumbling shit but they was just mad they couldn't get down. A few dudes didn't move. They didn't give a fuck what Monster was talking about. They was there to gamble and they would wait till somebody else got bank to get down or just sit on the side and bet on who's gonna roll a four or better.

"Five the point," Monster said after one of the Calvin brothers rolled and the number registered. Monster stepped up and head-cracked Lil Red. Regg went out, too.

Red bumped Regg when he was going to grab the dice and Regg ignored it because Red was reeking of Henny, but he felt where it was going.

"Sixty thou in it," the Calvin brother said. "What they down?"

"I'm down twenty," Red, Regg, and Monster said. The Calvin brother aced and had to pay everybody.

"A hundred thou in it. What they down?" the brother said, as if that sixty he just lost wasn't shit.

"I'm down forty," Monster said quickly.

"I'm down forty," Regg followed.

"I got the ends," Red said last.

The Calvin brother aced again. After he paid everybody, the brothers switched rollers and the other brother said, "A hundred thou in it. What they down?"

"Same bet," Regg said.

Monster said, "I'm down forty."

Red said, "I got the ends."

The other brother rolled and aced, also. He paid everybody then they said they were out. They knew when to call it quits. When both of them came out the gate weak they knew not to go too far. That's what made them smart.

Monster took over the bank and said, "What you down, Regg?" They was about to play head up because Monster wasn't going to gamble against Red. That was his family.

Regg said, "I'm good, Monster. I'm out," and threw him five stacks since he was the house and it was his spot.

"Nah, you good, Regg! I was in the game. I don't charge house rules when I'm in it," Monster said and threw the money back. Red intercepted it leaving Regg's hand in the air.

The whole place got silent. It was about to pop off.

"Now why would you do that?" Regg asked Red.

" 'Cause I can, you bitch! What the fuck you going to do about it?"

"Yo, chill, Red! Give that man his money. Regg is cool peoples," Monster butted in, knowing Red was drunk and upset about his brother.

"Fuck that, Monster! We got beef from the inside and we gonna settle it."

"You know what, Red? You got it. I don't want no beef with you. We out now and I ain't trying to go back. So let's leave it at that," Regg said.

"Yeah, that's what I thought, pussy," Lil Red said so the whole place heard. "You don't want no beef. Get the fuck outta here then. I'm keeping this li'l paper," Red said waving around Regg's knot of money.

Monster, wanting to defuse the situation, walked up to Regg, put his arm around his shoulder, and handed him more money than Regg gave him in the first place. He said, "My bad, Regg! This nigga trippin'. He just lost his brother. You know how that shit is."

While Monster was walking Regg out so he could leave without something jumping off, Lil Red yelled out, "Fuck all that! Tell that nigga suck my dick 'cause he's a bitch!"

Regg stopped in his tracks right before the doorway. "If I'm a bitch, put your gun and your mouth away and come outside. You the bitch! Nigga you ain't shit without your homeboys or a gun! And if you are, come out and prove it so I can beat your ass silly, you loudmouth coward!"

Lil Red was heated and stormed outside. He told himself he was going to stab Regg after he fucked him up.

"Let's go around the back so cops or nobody else don't break it up," Regg told Red.

"Let's go, nigga," Red accepted. "Nobody jumpin' nobody! This is a one on one," Red yelled out.

"Word up, nobody jumpin' nobody," Monster followed. Lil Red was his cousin and him and Regg were cool (they always used to gamble against each other); he was gonna keep it right. They got to the back and it was on. Everybody gave them space. It had been a long time since niggaz in the hood actually shot a fair one.

Lil Red and Regg both threw their hands up.

Lil Red said, "What up," and rushed into Regg bobbin' and weaving. He was a little faster than Regg had thought. Red hit once in the head and once in the body.

The crowd groaned, "Oooooooouuuuu!" It didn't rock Regg but it was enough to put him on point that Red had some skills. Regg had planned to use his height and reach to his advantage. Red tried to come in the same again on Regg. This time Regg sidestepped Red and caught him with two hard jabs to his left ear, which caused Red to stumble.

"Ooooooouuuuu," again from the crowd. Regg stepped closer to Red and caught him with another jab and an uppercut before he could recover from the stumble.

"Ooooouu!"

The blows hurt Red and he tried to scoop Regg to slam him but got another uppercut for his efforts. This one had him laid out on the ground.

"That's enough! That's enough, Regg," Monster said. "It's over. Y'all did it."

While Monster was holding Regg and telling him it was over, Lil Red fished in his pocket for his knife.

"Yo, he got a knife," somebody yelled. Regg and Monster turned to look at Lil Red who was coming full steam ahead toward them like a screaming bull; like Wolverine from the *X-Men*. Monster moved out of the way. He didn't like Regg enough to get in the way of a blade for him.

Red swung the blade upward. Regg tried to block it with his arms, but lost his footing and fell to the ground. Lil Red hopped on top of him and started poking Regg in his arms and his side while screaming "Motherfucker" with each thrust. Regg managed to catch Lil Red with a knee to the nuts. That stopped him. Red dropped the knife and Regg picked it up and shoved it into his neck. The whole crowd was shocked as fuck. It all happened so fast. It looked like Lil Red was killing Regg, then all of a sudden he was laying there dead with a knife in his neck.

Regg got off the ground bloodied up and ready to jet. He knew Lil Red's boys were gonna flip and try to kill him. Nobody gave chase. They were trying to tend to Lil Red.

The scene was too hot for the Calvin brothers. They hopped in the Benz they came in and got out of there to get a bite to eat and discuss their future plans.

"Listen, bro, I don't trust Albert anymore! He's not our real father anyway and he always treated our mother like shit," the younger brother said.

"Yeah, but he has always been good to us! He took us in knowing he wasn't our natural father. I don't feel that comfort-able with the idea of rubbing him out, baby bro," the older brother said. "And besides that, that guy Phil is a scumbag! As soon as Frank left his office talking about he didn't want to work with Phil anymore, that scumbag called us to kill him. That makes him even worse than Pops is! This whole 300 Crew shit is over anyway. Too many motherfuckers dead and the feds are scurrying around like roaches. When we go to see Pops I'm gonna try to convince him to retire and pass the torch to us. What's your thoughts?"

"Well, big brother, if he agrees, it's all good with me. But if he doesn't and he thinks we're gonna be his flunkies forever, he has another thing coming!"

The brothers drove in silence to Albert's house, never picking up on the fact that they were being followed by Frank. They got to the Murphy estate, which was about an hour and a half outside the city, and went straight inside. Their mother had just cooked dinner and was taking a nap. Albert was reading the paper.

The brothers were twenty-five and twenty-three and had been with Albert since they were seven and five. After his son Donald's mother passed, he met and married the brothers' mother and took the boys in as if they were his own. He raised them to be tough as nails and money earners just like he did his boy Donald. He always called them "my boys" because their dumb-ass father named both of them Calvin Kalvins.

"My boys, what goes on with you fellas?" Albert asked. "You haven't been home in days."

The older brother answered him. "Just bullshitting around. All the business is handled. All the books are good. Phil gave us a call a few days ago to let us know that guy Frank was leaving him. Too tired for this kind of business. I guess he wasn't a good recruit like you two thought he would be. We went to get him but he wasn't home. We'll go back in a few days."

The younger brother chimed in, "There's nothing we can do about Jake Billings. He killed CO Frazier his first day in so it is officially over for the 300!"

"And what are we doing about CO Frazier's loved ones?" Albert asked.

"He had no loved ones," the younger brother answered.

"I think you're wrong, my boy! Phil told me he was dating a nurse and I would like you to take care of that. No telling what he told her."

"Okay, no problem! I'll get the details and take care of it," the younger brother answered. "I'm going to chat with Mom. I'll talk to you later, Pops."

Albert looked at the older Calvin as the younger one walked away. "He thinks I don't see the resentment in his eyes," he said. "He is still like a baby! He wants to be the boss of everything without learning anything, but you have the brain to run the whole show. I know he is your baby brother and my boy but his attitude is beginning to irk me! He reminds me of Donald in so many ways. I believe if he didn't stay around you all the time he would be dead. But anyway, let's talk business, my boy. I'm going to hand everything over to you, not you and your brother, but you. You're going to be the one to have to explain to him why."

"Listen, Pops, he all right! He just gets emotional sometimes. I got him, don't worry about a thing," the older Calvin tried to explain.

All of a sudden, all the lights in the house went out, then came right back on, then went out again. Albert's instincts told him something was wrong. It was pitch black in the house.

"I'm going to turn the power back on," the younger Calvin yelled out and headed to the basement. He grabbed a flashlight out the kitchen drawer and ran down the steps. He flashed his light around to locate the box to hit the switches and found it. He thought he heard something and shined his light around behind him. "That you, bro?" He got no reply. He swept the light left and right and noticed the window in the basement was cracked open. That was strange because he had never seen that window open in the house as long as they had lived there. He reached for his gun but remembered he took it off and put it in the hallway closet like he and his brother always did. He knew someone was there with him. He could feel it. He kept spinning around, flashing the light around the room. He couldn't see anything, but he knew something was wrong. He began to head to the stairs and heard something behind him. He turned. The light landed on a face. It was Frank.

"Oh shit," the younger Calvin said, and those would be his last words.

Frank swung the short sword like a golf club in an upward motion and took all of the younger Calvin's facial features off with one swing—part of his chin, his lips, his nose, even most of his forehead. Frank could have actually made a Calvin mask, if he wanted to, with what was on the floor.

Frank then proceeded up the steps, but stopped before the top.

"Someone should be coming any second now," Frank said to himself.

"This motherfucker take long for everything," the older Calvin said, grabbing a flashlight out the kitchen drawer and heading toward the steps. Something made him stop. He went to the hallway closet to get his gun. Then he headed back to the basement steps. He ran down the stairs and flashed his light. "Yo, bro, where you at? Yo, bro, stop playing!" He tripped and landed in something wet. When he shined his light at the floor he couldn't believe what he was seeing. It was his little brother he'd tripped over and it was his blood that was wet on his hands.

The older brother sprang to his feet, flashed the light around, and headed back to the steps. He got to the top, but it was too late. Frank had locked him in the basement and wedged a chair up against the door.

Albert Murphy had his .38 out waiting. He heard three gun-shots and got nervous. It was the older Calvin trying to shoot the lock off the door. He couldn't bust it open because of the chair Frank wedged against it. Albert Murphy tried to run but tripped over Frank who was standing right behind him.

"Where you going, Albert?" Frank asked.

"What do you want with me? I have done nothing to you. Leave me alone! Who are you?"

Frank laughed and Albert shot off every round in his .38 very recklessly, not hitting a thing.

"You don't even know who I am. You don't know if you did something to me or not," Frank said.

"Who are you then?" Albert asked.

"It's me, Frank! The guy that worked for Phil and quit. The guy that your two sons came after."

"What does this have to do with me? I didn't send my sons after you. It was Phil."

"Oh, I figured that," Frank answered.

"So why me? Why not get Phil?"

"Because you're a scumbag, too, and you have been fucking up the city and the youth for years! So I figured I would do a good deed and get rid of you. Don't worry about Phil. He's gonna get his, too! By the way, I killed one of your boys so you will have some company where you're going," Frank told him.

"Can I ask you a question?" Albert asked.

"What?" Frank was curious.

"How can you see in the dark?"

"Black belt shit." Then Frank shoved the sword deep into Albert's belly, pulling all of his guts out with it. Then he cut straight across his throat.

Frank ran outside when he was done. He thought he was scot-free as he drove away in his Mustang. He never considered the fact that the feds were posted up watching Albert Murphy.

Frank had just went and killed two men that were under surveillance. Everything that Frank did, he would have to go to jail for. He drove a few miles and stopped to get gas and take a leak. Before he could exit the gas station bathroom they came in and got him.

"Freeze! Get down on the ground! One wrong move and I'll blow your fucking brains out!"

Frank wanted to shoot it out with the police, but he decided against it. He wasn't with killing the people who upheld the law. That would make him no better than the slime balls he just killed. He got down on the floor, got cuffed, and was on his way to jail.

The Murphy household wasn't the only place the feds had

their eye on. They'd witnessed the entire altercation at Monster's place and followed Regg to the emergency room, where he'd just finished getting stitched up. He had been stabbed seventeen times. Something in his head was telling him not to go to the hospital, but he was bleeding too bad and had too many holes, so he had no choice. As soon as the doctors were finished with him he heard, "Don't move. Put your hands in the air!"

CHAPTER 23

MR. INVINCIBLE

Two days later

Jake wasn't in the hospital for long. The cell block they threw him back into looked like it had been shut down since the seventies and was only used from time to time to teach inmates a lesson. He didn't see or hear anyone but himself.

"See how you like it down here, motherfucker," one of the COs told him.

The other one laughed. "Yeah, I bet this nigga don't be so tough down here." He smashed his elbow into Jake's rib cage.

They brought Jake to the last cell in the ancient cell block, uncuffed him, and threw him in. Before they left him, the CO who had smashed him in the ribs said, "You don't look so tough to me, punk."

Jake knew better than to say anything stupid. He tried to

save his ass by telling the COs, "Yo, I don't think I'm tough and I don't want no problems. That was personal and I did what I had to so I can stay alive."

"I don't even give a fuck, punk," the CO who had hit Jake replied. Then he smashed Jake in the ribs again. This time with five blows that curled Jake over. Then he elbowed Jake in the back, forcing him to hit the floor. "Come on and get up and try to break my neck! Come on, punk," the CO yelled out.

"Yo, calm down," the other CO told his partner. "What the fuck is wrong with you? You trying to get fired? Well I ain't. So do that shit on your own time!" After he said that, they left Jake in the deserted, decrepit cell block by himself.

Jake knew he was fucked. Having beef with the police is one of the worst things that can happen to a man in jail. Jake had nothing and no one to talk to besides God.

"Father, I know I have done a lot of wrong and foul acts in my lifetime and I'm gonna have to pay for them one way or the other. I just ask that one day you see it fit to forgive me, Father, and let me get to heaven after I finish doing my time in hell. I also ask that you bless my child and her mother in abundance."

Jake's conversations with God were getting deeper and deeper as the weeks went by. He wasn't sure how long he was down there because there was no way to tell time without a clock. There were no windows, so he didn't know whether it was light or dark outside. What he did do is count how many times the police came in and whipped his ass. He was on his ninth beating. He thought he ate or attempted to eat around a total of fifteen times. He was assuming he had been down there for a month. He decided to stop worrying about time. He med-itated to keep from going insane, remembering some of the materials Old Nebbie taught him, trying to stay strong however he could. He repeated songs he loved and thought of movies he loved to entertain himself. Sometimes he stared at the one little lightbulb that was flickering in the hallway.

Before long, Jake was doing at least two thousand sit-ups and two thousand push-ups and dips per day. He told himself there were jails in other parts of the world ten times worse than what he was in. Those prisoners barely ever ate and if they didn't break, why would he? He would make the best out of his situation and use the peace and quiet time to elevate his mind to a place it never reached before. He would live a whole different life in his mind. His body was just a shell sitting in jail, but his mind and soul could travel the world and the seven seas, even to the sun and moon if he wanted. So if they planned on breaking him down with a dark, decrepit room like a slave in a dungeon, they had another thing coming. He would rebuild himself to be something and someone too deep for them to understand. He would truly be Mr. Invincible.

There was a saying from the Good Book he liked to recite. "The Lord is my helper; I will not be afraid. What can man do to me?"

He had been in the dungeon for nine months, almost ten. The beatings had stopped a long time ago—due to prayer, Jake believed. They already gave him his slop for the day, so when Jake heard a guard approaching, he was curious as to what was happening.

"Today is your lucky day, you son of a bitch," the guard stated as he stopped at his cell. "You know why? You got court today, that's why! You get to go upstairs, use the real shower in a real cell block, and you even get to change your jail jumpsuit.

They might let you get a sip from the water fountain instead of your old nasty sink. Does real water even come out of that thing?" the guard asked without caring about the answer. "You might even get to eat a tray that ain't been spit in!"

Jake didn't bother to answer back or be bothered with what the clown CO was saying. He saw the spit in his food plenty of times. He either had to run his food under his nasty sink water, which was tinted green, or he would give it to his other cell mates, which were the rats and roaches.

"Come on, hurry up and move. You ain't got all day," the CO ordered.

Jake was brought to a cell block where everybody was asleep and locked in. The CO gave him a bar of soap, white boxers, a T-shirt and socks with some new oranges, a shaving kit, a toothbrush and toothpaste. Jake shaved, brushed and re-brushed his teeth, and took as long as he could in the shower.

After thirty minutes, the guard had to yell, "Get the fuck outta there. We gotta go."

When Jake came out of the shower dressed, the C.O. shackled him. His legs and his arms were cuffed to his waist belt. They were doing him like they did all cop killers and mass murderers and anyone they considered a threat. Jake was supposed to be transported to court in a single squad car, but they were all out being used. So he had to get on the bus everyone else was using for court.

The bus was packed. Jake didn't bother to scan the metal box on wheels to see who was who or what was what. He didn't even care. His mind was in a totally different zone. The CO ordered Jake to sit in the first row, alone, then sat in the row behind him with his shotgun in his hand. Jake had not seen daylight in almost a year. It felt good to look at the sun and the clouds.

He heard the whispers of, "Oh shit! That nigga's still here."

"I thought they killed him."

"Told you he wasn't in the feds, nigga!"

Jake ignored it all. Today he just wanted to appreciate looking out of the window and seeing something different. Jake got to court and was put in a separate holding cell from everyone else.

An unenthused court-appointed lawyer came in the back and told Jake, "Listen, we're gonna try to get you life. The DA is gonna be talking the death penalty."

Jake cut him off. "Just tell them you don't want to drag this on. I'll plead guilty today and I want to be sentenced as soon as possible."

The lawyer told Jake: "It's not going to go like that. We have procedures and certain protocols we have to follow."

"Yeah, okay," Jake said.

When Jake got called in front of the judge, he let the DA say his piece. Before Jake's lawyer could get a word in, Jake said, "Excuse me, Your Honor. I would like to address the court with something."

"I usually don't do this, but go ahead Mr. Billings."

"Well, Your Honor, I just want to say that I don't want to waste the taxpayer's money, your time, the District Attorney's time, or my time. No disrespect to the process of the federal court, but I would like to plead guilty on every count today and be sentenced to whatever it is I'm going to be sentenced to as soon as possible, whether it's life or death, Your Honor. And one other thing, Your Honor. The circumstances I'm being held under are not humane. I'm aware I am locked in the only correctional facility that holds federal inmates in the area, but I'm being treated like an animal due to the fact I killed CO Frazier. But that doesn't mean I should be subjected to eating food with spit in it and living in a cell with inadequate water. I am aware of the fact that even though it's a local jail, you can be held there up to four years. I ask to please make sure that doesn't happen to me. Please, Your Honor!"

The judge told Jake he heard him and would make sure things went as speedy as possible. Then he called the lawyers to approach the bench. Jake overheard the judge tell the DA that his living conditions better be fixed. Then the DA mentioned something about Jake killing Frazier. Then Jake's lawyer mentioned something to the likes of CO Frazier was being investigated due to his criminal activity. Jake couldn't hear anything else. The lawyers returned and court was adjourned.

Jake prayed that what he did would work and if it didn't, he would just make the best of his situation. Jake rode back to the jail. When he got there he was unshackled and thrown in the bullpen with everyone else. He thanked God for taking care of his problem. He knew they weren't going to put him back in the dungeon.

Jake was put in the bullpen with twenty-two other dudes. Now it was just him left. They was trying to hit him with a dose of bullpen therapy but that wasn't shit to what he had just been through. He actually didn't mind what they were doing.

Meanwhile, upstairs in the federal part of the jail, "That shit is true niggaz been saying all day. That nigga is still in here. I seen him with my own eyes," one of Regg's homies was telling him, as he stopped at the law library to kick it with Regg.

"When I was leaving the kitchen and walking by the bullpen I seen the nigga just sittin' in there. Something looks different about him! I can't explain it, though."

Regg closed the book he was reading. "I heard they had that nigga in the dungeon, but I thought niggaz was bullshittin'. That shit been closed for years. You mean to tell me they held that man in a part of the jail nobody has been in for years? I bet we would look like there was something different about us, too, if that shit happened!"

"Yo, Regg, you think it's going to pop off with Jake, Frankie, and Clips?" Regg's man asked.

"How could it not, my man? How could it not?"

In another part of the jail, Clips walked to his homeboy's cell. "Yo Frank, you know our friend Mr. Invincible is back, right?"

Frank laid in his bunk reading the paper. He answered his good friend without putting it down, "Yeah I know. Been hearing that since this morning. So it was true he has been in this jail the whole time, so what!"

Clips said, "The so what is that he will be upstairs tomorrow, or possibly even late tonight, and I wanna know what you want to do with him. I mean we did almost kill the man before. He might be a little upset over that, not that we give a fuck, but I like being on point and having my schedule right. So if killing him is on the schedule, let me know."

"Clips, we ain't killing him," Frank said. "Unless he tries to kill us. Other than that, we're chilling."

A CO finally came over to Jake and said, "Come on." He handed him a bedroll and a bullpen sandwich when he let him out of the bullpen.

"Where to?" Jake asked. "Back to the dungeon?"

"Nah, you headed to the federal side."

"Okay, that's a big step up from where I was at," Jake said to himself.

"Now you look out for yourself in there," the officer told him.

"You know something I should know?" Jake asked.

The guard looked at Jake with raised eyebrows. "You don't know, do you?"

"Know what?" Jake asked.

"Listen," the guard said. "They're sending you upstairs to the federal side. That's where all your enemies are. The two dudes that put you in a coma are over there. Ike and Cory are over there and every other nigga you probably got into it with."

Jake said, "Oh well, it is what it is."

When Jake got to his cell block, it was 9:30, half an hour away from lock in. He looked around the house and didn't spot any threats. He walked to his cell to put his bag down. Then he went and stood by his doorway and looked around. He decided to go hit the pull-up bar he saw when he walked into the block. It was the standard pull up/dip/push-up machine you saw in every jail. It had been a long time since Jake hit the bar. He couldn't do that when he was down in the dungeon.

All eyes were on him. Some niggaz were curious on how he even made it back to population. Some of them were curious to how he was even alive. Some thought he was sent to another jail. Jake really didn't give a fuck what any of them thought. His main concern was to keep his mind and body right. He had lost weight since he was in the dungeon, but he was still all muscle from the push-ups and sit-ups and dips off the bed he had been doing. Jake made his first two sets of pull-ups fifty clips 'cause he knew niggaz was watching him. He had to let them know the strength was still there. Then he just did a few twenty clips after that.

Jake looked at the clock and saw that it was a few minutes from lock in, so he walked back to his cell and stood by his doorway to observe who's and what type of house he was dealing with. He took a deep breath to mentally prepare himself to deal with the nonsense of being surrounded by liars, dirty motherfuckers, gangsters, fake gangsters, drug addicts, homosexuals, undercover homosexuals, gamblers, COs, and all the other hustlers, killers, and strong-arm robbers.

Jake heard the five-minutes-to-lock-in bell and looked up at the clock. He couldn't believe his eyes. It was Regg coming through the cell block door. Regg spotted Jake at the same time. A sudden nervousness came over Regg and he gave Jake a "what's up" head nod that he instantly regretted when Jake just looked at him, turned around, and went in his cell. The door slammed shut behind him.

"Motherfucking coward," Jake said to himself.

"Damn, I have to deal with this nigga," Regg said before the cell doors slammed shut.

———

"Phil Rosenberg is on top of the world, babies! You rolling with the best," Phil said like he was a star athlete or a champion of something. Phil was talking shit on the penthouse balcony to three of his lady friends he decided to hang out with. Phil's idea of hanging out was a big duplex suite at a high-class hotel with an eight ball of coke, some E pills, some good weed, and vodka and tequila.

"Listen, ladies, I got two friends coming over. I want y'all to show them a nice time, but that's later on. For now I need y'all to clean this shit up and put the drugs away. As a matter of fact, leave all this shit right here! Damn, I'm high as a kite! I'm going downstairs. Don't interrupt me unless I call one of y'all! I'm hopping in the shower for a while."

Phil had a meeting with the remaining Calvin brother and Monster. After taking his shower, he didn't feel like going back up the stairs to change. He yelled upstairs, "One of you ladies bring my clothes down here and lay them out on the bed! I'm going to fix me a drink."

Phil was at the bar making his drink when he heard one of the girls run down the steps. Without looking at her he asked, "You got all of my shit?"

"No, Phil, I don't have all your shit!"

Phil jerked around to see M.B. standing there holding a gun on him.

"What the fuck are you doing here, you fucking cunt?"

"So disrespectful when I have a gun in my hand, Phil?"

"Bitch, you never shot or killed anything in your life and I'm pretty sure you don't want to go to jail now. Where the fuck did you send my bitches, M.B.?"

"They went home, Phil, like I told them to. Did you forget I'm the one who hooked you up with most of your connects, even the one who sends you your hoes, dumb ass?"

"Cut the shit, M.B., and get to the point! I got a meeting in a couple of minutes and I wouldn't want one of them to come in here and see you with that gun out and put a bullet in your pretty li'l head now," Phil said.

"I know you have a meeting with Calvin and Monster, Phil. I have been following you for a few weeks now, but neither one of those gentlemen will be showing up. The girls won't be coming back, either."

"And why's that?" Phil was starting to get a little nervous, but he didn't let it show.

"Because they all know about you now. So will Jake. I wrote him a letter explaining the whole thing. He should be getting it any day now."

"What the fuck are you talking about, M.B.?"

"You know, Phil, it took some time to figure it out, but I did," M.B. said. "You are the one who set up Jake's store to get robbed in the first place. Your intentions were to discourage him from being around. You hoped that robbery would leave him broke and make him relocate. Couldn't bear the fact he witnessed you get raped. So when he went to jail you went and told Albert about Jake killing his son and his friends, but you made it seem like I got raped and you wasn't there. But you never expected Albert to work so hard on getting Jake killed. You didn't expect him to want to be the one to hurt Jake personally. When he decided to go in on the inside and have your guys' other partner, Frazier, help him, that's when you went into extra hard mode and went to the jail. You hired Franklin Butler to do the job, which he almost did. That's around the time you told me Jake was out and just left town. But Jake didn't die. Instead, he fell into a coma. You probably wanted to kill him in the hospital, but you couldn't afford to make yourself hot. Then somehow you got in Kim's head. You told her about my baby. You scared her with talk of fed time, being she was the founder of the 300 and Jake's girl. Then came your death threat for her to let you know if Jake ever got up; if she didn't, that was it for someone in her family. She actually believed you until your men tried to kill her, too. When you knew you couldn't count on her anymore because you double-crossed her, you got Mitch in on it. You wanted him to kill his nephew, but he wouldn't or couldn't do it. He was actually trying to save Jake's life. That's why he killed Kim and not Jake. Mitch didn't know Nine-One was a fed and he was about to bring you down, so you got real lucky when he got killed. You are a lowlife! You were trying to get Jake killed because you knew the feds were on to him killing Phat Murphy. At first I thought it was really over me, but that ain't the case. You didn't want the feds to get Jake for them bodies because you didn't want the feds to hear the whole story. The reason why you didn't want them to hear it is because you are a motherfucking federal agent! And you didn't want your fellow agents to knock you off. You didn't want them to know you got fucked up the ass. You're not only a fed, but you're a dirty one that has made money off your cover!"

Phil turned red as a beet. He had blood in his eyes. "Fuck you, you fucking whore," Phil screamed. "How the fuck did you find all this out?"

"I kinda stumbled upon it, Phil. When I saw that Nine-One was a fed, I just automatically assumed he was on Jake's case. Then I thought about it. He had more than enough time and evidence to bring Jake in. He was trying to get closer to the 300 Crew. He knew Kim started it, but when he found out you were in it and that wasn't part of your cover or case agenda, he was on to you. But now that he is dead and most of the Crew is dead, and because Jake and your friend Frank are in jail, you think you got off scot-free."

"You still ain't say exactly how you stumbled on all of this, M.B."

"When you got my address, Phil, you fucked up! You fucked up bad! How did you get it? You went to my real estate agent and gave my name and picture and told him I was under federal investigation. You got my address from him, that was your mistake. You fucked up! My real estate agent is an ATF agent and I used to be an ATF agent, too."

Phil was speechless. She had him. He wished he could kick himself in the ass. It made so much sense. What other way could she have had so much info on that many people for so many years? No wonder she just up and left. How come he hadn't looked into her background deeper?

"So what the fuck are you doing? You gonna take me in? Then come on over here and cuff me." Phil stuck his hands out.

"No, Phil. I ain't here to arrest you. I said I used to be an ATF agent. I was forced into early retirement for being a dirty cop like you, but I was nowhere near as grimy as you! Yeah, I stole and had a baby by Jake while I was investigating Kim, so I had to leave my job."

Phil sensed M.B. was going to shoot him and tried to throw a liquor bottle. She sidestepped and put a bullet in Phil's groin.

"That's for me, motherfucker!" Then she shot him again in his stomach. "That one is for Jake, motherfucker!" Then she shot him in the head. "That's for my daughter and making her grow up without a father."

M.B. left Phil in his hotel room sprawled out bleeding.

Regg knew he had to be well prepared to fuck with Jake. He also knew Jake just got in the house and most likely he didn't have a blade on him. So if he ran up first, he could get Jake.

Jake was in his cell thinking of how to make the best out of his time. He would tell Regg in the morning to just stay away from him. He didn't have a plan for Frank and Clips and he knew he would definitely see them in the yard or mess hall. "Whatever happens, happens," he told himself.

Morning time came and Jake was up. He couldn't sleep. He was waiting for the lock-out bell to ring. He knew Regg might try his hand and it was going to be an early morning wreck.

The lock-out bell rang and Jake stepped out of his cell. Regg stepped out of his, and so did the rest of the block. The CO made the chow call and everybody who was hungry headed to the mess hall. Some fell back 'cause they was too tired. Some fell back because they were gonna eat some shit off their commissary.

Jake headed to the mess hall. He made sure to play the wall of the hallway as he walked. Regg was kind of nervous-looking but trying to cover it up with a poker face. That was making Jake uneasy. As soon as Jake picked a spot where he could eat and observe everything, he got on line for his food. He made a mental note that Regg was ten men behind the guy that was behind him. Jake's spot was somebody else's table, but the kids it belonged to noticed it was Jake in the spot and kept moving. So Jake ended up with the whole table to himself. As Jake was eating, he noticed Clips walking into the mess hall, which made him reminisce on his brutal beating.

222 | STYLES P

Clips noticed it got quiet as soon as he entered. The tension was extremely thick. He scanned the area and saw Jake sitting by himself. Clips not giving a fuck, got his tray, cut the breakfast line, and joined Jake for breakfast.

"Good morning, Jake," Clips said, as if he and Jake were the best friends in the world and he never played a part in trying to kill him.

Jake replied, "You're a funny guy!"

Frank had walked into the mess hall and knew something was going down. He saw Clips sitting with Jake at a table by themselves. He skipped getting his tray, went straight to the table they were sitting at, and sat down next to Clips.

"Clips, what are you doing?" Frank asked as soon as he got to the table.

"Just saying good morning, that's all, Frank."

"Yo, check this out," Frank was addressing Jake. "Let's just squash the beef."

"I can do that if you two go back to your cell block and go to sleep for two years. Do that and we call it even," Jake said.

"Listen, Jake, you can play tough, but you don't stand a chance against us. I'm trying to be levelheaded, but I see we gonna have to handle our business," Frank said.

"I prefer it that way," Jake said. "One way or the other y'all gonna have to pay, you know. I ain't letting that shit slide."

As soon as Jake said slide, Clips hopped over the table with his blade out. That was exactly what Jake expected him to do. Jake hopped up and smashed his tray into Clips' throat and stepped back. He knew Clips was hurt bad. Frank walked around the table and Jake threw his hands up. Frank kicked Jake in his knee and made him buckle. Then he caught him with a kick in the side of the head that dropped Jake to the floor. Jake's head was ringing, but he jumped to his feet fast. Frank threw another kick at Jake's ribs, but Jake caught his leg and slammed Frank to the floor. Jake felt Frank's strength and knew Frank was some kind of expert in something. Jake tried to stomp Frank's leg and Frank ended up sweeping his leg and hopping up. Jake hopped up just as fast. They were squared back up and Frank kicked Jake in the mouth and hit him twice in the body. Jake didn't know if the body shot was a fist or foot, but he knew a rib was broken and he was dizzy.

Clips got back up and tried to hop back into the action, but Regg pushed him away and said, "One on one, he is already losing. So this gonna be fair!"

"Fuck you, nigga," Clips told Regg and tried to poke him, but Clips was slow. His equilibrium still wasn't right from when the tray hit his throat. So Regg sidestepped his half-ass swing and dug into his ass quick with four blows. Clips hit the floor with a bloodied-up grill.

Frank and Jake were practically the same height and weight, but everybody watching could tell Frank clearly outclassed Jake in fighting style. Jake was tired and he was trying to get his bearings, but Frank was overwhelming him. Frank hit him with a four piece. Jake tried to rush Frank to slam him, but Frank put him in a choke hold that was putting Jake to sleep. Everybody watching, who thought Jake was a bad man, thought Frank was something terrible.

Frank felt Jake going to sleep in his arms and began to squeeze tighter. Frank decided he was going to choke Jake to death. He knew if he didn't, Jake would keep coming back.

Jake knew he was about to die. His life was flashing before

his eyes. He dug deep down and thought about his daughter and found the strength to lift Frank over his back while he was still in the choke hold. He had seen it in a wrestling match when he was younger. He suplexed Frank while Frank was still choking him, forcing Frank to let go of the choke hold. Jake sprung to his feet again and shot a two piece at Frank and Frank blocked both of them. Frank reached into his pants and pulled out a blade. Jake had no blade and Regg tried to throw Jake his, but Frank intercepted it in midair and threw it at Jake. It landed in Jake's chest. Frank threw it with so much force and so perfectly, Jake felt like the blade went through him—but it didn't, it was stuck in him. Only the handle stuck out of his chest.

Frank smirked at Jake. Then he rushed him and stabbed him in his gut hard three times. It was over and everybody knew it. Frank, Regg, even Clips—who wasn't dead but was leaking bad—and the CO, who had seen enough and decided to pull the plug, saw Jake hit the floor.

Frank started to walk away until he heard Jake speak. "Hey bitch! That's all you got? Don't you know I'm Mr. Invincible?" Jake got to his feet blood and all.

Frank looked at Jake with total disbelief and gripped his knife tight. He walked toward Jake. Frank told himself he was gonna slit Jake's throat from ear to ear, guaranteed death. Frank got closer to Jake, who looked like he was gonna die any second with that knife handle sticking out his chest. For a second Frank had to admire Jake. He was a throwback, a true warrior. He looked like he didn't mind dying this way.

Frank was three footsteps from Jake, about to send him to his maker, when Jake grabbed the knife handle that was in his chest and pulled it out. Blood shot out like his chest was a sprinkler. Jake used every last little bit of strength he had to successfully stab Frank in the esophagus. He twisted the blade around and yanked it out. Frank never even had a chance to take his final blow. He grabbed his throat and fell to the floor choking on his own blood. He died gasping for air with Jake standing over him.

Jake looked around the mess hall. He was dizzy. Then his focus became clear. He was breathing hard. He had a strong feeling they would be his last breaths. He was bleeding from the mouth with half of his guts out and a couple of teeth missing. He looked around at every face in the mess hall with the intensity of a dying president or religious leader taking one last look at his followers. He threw his right fist up and said, "Invincible," then he dropped to the floor.

ACKNOWLEDGMENTS

I would like to acknowledge all those who helped me on the book. Kristi Clifford and Asti Management, Danielle Scott, and Scott Mason.

Thanks to Porscha Burke and Kara Olsen for helping with the edits.

Thanks to Nikki Turner for giving me this opportunity. Melody Guy, Craig Robinson, Cousin Rodney Styles, Hit, Sheek, Kiss, and Bizzy.

Thanks to Jaja and Naser for helping me put the book together.

Thanks to all my family and friends who supported me on this. There are too many names to mention.

I would also like to say what's up to all those in jail. Stay strong, work out your body and mind.

And a big shout out to all those who read . . . point blank period.

ABOUT THE AUTHOR

STYLES P (David Styles), a Queens-born, Yonkers-bred emcee, first stepped onto the scene as one-third of the famed hip-hop trio the LOX (aka D-Block), a group he formed with childhood friends Jadakiss and Sheek. After guest-starring on multiplatinum singles like "We'll Always Love Big Poppa," and "All About the Benjamins," Styles and the LOX released their albums *Money, Power & Respect* and *We Are the Streets,* before the group's members began focusing on solo projects. Styles P's solo recording projects include *A Gangster and a Gentleman, Time Is Money,* and *Super Gangster (Extraordinary Gentleman). Invincible* is his first novel.

The soundtrack to

INVINCIBLE

is available at
www.StylesP.net